新概念英语2
同步口语拓展练习

王 月等 编著

U0133092

中国水利水电出版社
www.waterpub.com.cn

内 容 提 要

本书依据《新概念英语》(第二册),以课为单位进行有针对性地口语练习,能够增强读者学习兴趣,提高听、说能力。

本书适用于学习《新概念英语》(第二册)的读者。

图书在版编目(CIP)数据

新概念英语2同步口语拓展练习 / 王月等编著. —北京:
中国水利水电出版社,2008
ISBN 978 - 7 - 5084 - 5903 - 5

Ⅰ. 新… Ⅱ. 王… Ⅲ. 英语—口语—习题 Ⅳ. H319.9-44

中国版本图书馆 CIP 数据核字(2008)第 145415 号

书　　名	新概念英语2同步口语拓展练习
作　　者	王月 等 编著
出版发行	中国水利水电出版社(北京市三里河路6号　100044) 网址:www.waterpub.com.cn E-mail:sales@waterpub.com.cn 电话:(010) 63202266(总机)、68367658(营销中心)
经　　售	北京科水图书销售中心(零售) 电话:(010) 88383994、63202643 全国各地新华书店和相关出版物销售网点
排　　版	贵艺图文设计中心
印　　刷	北京市地矿印刷厂
规　　格	145mm×210mm　32 开本　10.625 印张　392 千字
版　　次	2008 年 11 月第 1 版　2008 年 11 月第 1 次印刷
印　　数	0001—5000 册
定　　价	**23.80** 元

凡购买我社图书,如有缺页、倒页、脱页的,本社营销中心负责调换

新概念英语 2
同步口语拓展练习

主　编　王　月

编　委　王　月　　段其刚　　彭乃鹏　　丁　静
　　　　庞天翔　　黄　毅　　刘翠楠　　曹　畅
　　　　郭丽萍　　王福强　　王文敏　　郑崑琳
　　　　韩利俊　　陈轶斐　　郑　炎　　郭　丹
　　　　郭宗炎　　侯卫群　　刘　洋　　艾　静

Contents

目录

A private conversation
私人谈话

I Use the word (s) to make sentence (s)

Theater

_____.

Theater — seat

_____.

Go to — theater — seat

_____.

Plant

_____.

Plant — garden

_____.

Plant — garden — yesterday

_____.

Private

_____.

Private — patient

_____.

Private — patient — hospital

_____.

II Practice the key patterns

T: he — go to the theater — last week

S1: When did he go to the theater?

S2: He went to the theater last week.

S3: Last week he went to the theater.

S4: Did he go to the theater last week?

Practise: (1) I — read a newspaper — today

(2) my mother — watch TV — this evening

(3) Xiao Ming — clean the classroom — this morning

(4) they — have a meeting — last week

T: I could not hear the actors.

S1: Why did you get very angry?

S2: What did you hear in the theater?

S3: I could not hear the actor at all.

Practise: (1) I didn't enjoy this film.

(2) He hurried off the washroom.

(3) Kate turned around and cried loudly.

(4) She likes listening to some light music.

III Retell the story

Firstly complete the blanks and remember what you said.

Last week I went to the _____. I had a very good seat. The play was very _____. I did not enjoy it. A young man and a young woman were _____. They were talking loudly. I got very angry. _____. I turned a round. I looked at the man and the woman angrily. They did not _____. In the end, I could not _____ it. I turned round again. 'I can't hear a word!' I said angrily.

'It's none of your _____,' the young man said rudely.
'This is a _____!'
Secondly retell the story in the third person.

IV Active questions

1. Where did you go last week?
2. Did you have a good seat?
3. What about the play?
4. Did you enjoy it?
5. Who were sitting behind you?
6. What were they talking about?
7. Could you hear it?
8. How did you look at the man and the women when you turned around?
9. What did they reply?

2

Breakfast or lunch?
早餐还是午餐?

I Use the word (s) to make sentence (s)

Never

_____

Never — get up

_____

Never — get up — Sunday

_____

Sometimes

_____ .

Sometimes — stay in bed

_____ .

Sometimes — stay in bed — until

_____ .

Telephone

_____ .

Telephone — ring

_____ .

Telephone — ring — dark

_____ .

II Practice the key patterns

T: his father — die — come back.

S1: His father didn't die until he came back.

S2: His father was alive until he came back.

Practice:（1）I — do my homework — come in

（2）he — draw the picture — lunchtime

（3）Andy — get up — ring

（4）Xiaoming — speak loudly/quietly — lose her temper

T: jog — in the park — now

S1: John is jogging in the park now.

S2: What is John doing?

S3: Is John jogging in the park?

S4: Where is John jogging now?

Practice:（1）have a shower — in the bathroom — now

（2）play football — in the playground — now

（3）drive the car — on the road — at the moment

（4）water the flowers — in the garden — now

T: Peter — late for school — often

S1: Peter is often late for school.

S2: How often is Peter late for school?

Practice:（1）Susan — help her mother water the flowers — sometimes

（2）they — wash the dishes — always

（3）Kate — go to school by bus — rarely

（4）she — go to see the film with her classmates — always

（5）her sister — make mistakes — frequently

III Retell the story

Firstly complete the blanks and remember what you said.

It was Sunday. I never get up early _____. I sometimes stay in bed until _____. Last Sunday I _____ _____ very late. I _____. It was dark outside. 'What a day!' I thought. 'It's raining again.' Just then, the telephone _____. It was my aunt Lucy. 'I've just arrived by train,' she said. 'I'm coming to see you.'

'But I'm still having breakfast,' I said.

'_____?' she asked.

'I'm having breakfast,' I repeated.

'Dear me,' she said. '_____? It's one o'clock!'

Secondly retell the story in the third person.

IV Active questions

1. What day was it?
2. Do you often get up early on Sundays?
3. Do you ever get up before lunchtime?
4. What was it like outside?
5. When I was looking out of the window, what happened?
6. Who telephoned you?
7. What did she say?
8. What did you answer?
9. Was your aunt surprised at what you answered or not?
10. What was the actual time?

Lesson 3

Please send me a card
请给我寄一张明信片

I Use the word (s) to make sentence (s)

Visit

_____ .

Visit — museum

_____ .

Visit — museum — holiday

_____ .

Send

_____ .

Send — postcard

_____ .

Send — postcard — friend

_____ .

Single tree

_____ .

Single tree — stand

_____ .

Single tree — stand — sun

_____ .

II Practice the key patterns

T: read a book — but — understand

S1: What did you do?

S2: I read a book just now.

S3: I read a book but I didn't understand one word at all.

Practice: (1) like animals — but — hurt

(2) help you — but — break

(3) fall down — but — hurt

(4) fix the chair — but — work

T: want — see — by bus

S1: What do you want to do?

S2: I want to see Rose in hospital by bus.

Practice: (1) like — go to school — on foot

(2) hope — attend the meeting — by taxi

(3) want — play basketball — by subway

(4) love — visit my aunt — by bus

T: lend — my sister — a knife

S1: What did he lend your sister?

S2: He lent my sister a knife.

Practice: (1) lend — him — a dictionary

(2) borrow — us — a bike

(3) give — them — presents

(4) show — her — beautiful photos

III Retell the story

Firstly complete the blanks and remember what you said.

Postcards always _____ my holidays. Last summer, I went to Italy. I visited _____ and _____. A friendly waiter taught me a few words of Italian. Then he ＿＿＿＿＿ me a book. I read a few lines, but ＿＿＿＿＿＿＿＿＿. Every day I ＿＿＿＿＿＿＿ postcards. My holidays passed quickly, but I did not ＿＿＿＿＿ cards to my friends. On the last day I made a ＿＿＿＿ ＿＿＿＿. I got up early and bought thirty-seven cards. I ＿＿＿＿ ＿＿＿＿＿＿ in my room, but I did not write a ＿＿＿＿ card!

Secondly retell the story in the third person.

Ⅳ Active questions

1. What always spoils your holidays?
2. How did you spend your holidays?
3. Could you speak Italian?
4. Who taught you?
5. What did he lend you?
6. Was the book difficult?
7. Did you send any cards to your friends?
8. What did you do on the last day?
9. How many cards did you buy?
10. Where did you stay all day?

Ⅴ Translation

1. 别扫兴。
2. 你不应该惯孩子。
3. 我想就这个话题再说几句。
4. 我可以和你说句话吗？
5. 我可以管你借些钱吗？
6. 有些人既不向人借钱也不借钱给别人。
7. 海滩上一个人也没有。
8. 他借给我一本书。

9. 他寄给我一张卡片。

10. 请再给他一次机会。

11. 他给儿子带回来一样礼物。

12. 你能替我买几张邮票吗?

13. 她给我做了一份早餐。

14. 他的叔叔给他留了一些钱。

15. 她给她的朋友看了看她新买的衣服。

Lesson 4

An exciting trip
激动人心的旅行

I Use the word(s) to make sentence(s)

Receive

_____ .

Receive — Australia

_____ .

Receive — Australia — before

_____ .

Engineer

_____ .

Engineer — worker

_____ .

Engineer — worker — company

_____ .

Enjoy

_____ .

Enjoy — yourself

_____ .

Enjoy — yourself — trip

_____ .

II Practice the key patterns

T: she — in American — two years

S1: How long has she been in American?

S2: She has been in American for two years.

S3: Has she gone to American?

S4: Has she been to American?

Practice: (1) they — in Australia — a long time

(2) he — there — one month

(3) I — keep the antique — many years

(4) Susan — study — four years

T: feel — trip — interesting

S1: I feel this trip very interesting.

S2: Oh, what an interesting trip!

Practice: (1) believe — plan — important

(2) hear — film — instructive

(3) see — picture — colorful

(4) make — meeting — tedious

T: you — spend — evenings

S1: How do you usually spend your evenings?

S2: I invite some friends to my home.

Practice: (1) English people — celebrate — New Year's Day

(2) we — get to — Shanghai Museum

(3) they — call — your parents

(4) he — spend — summer holiday

III Retell the story

Firstly complete the blanks and remember what you said.

I have just _____ from my brother, Tim. He

is in Australia. He _____ for six months. Tim is
an engineer. He is working for a big _____ and he has already
visited a great number of _____ in Australia. He has just
bought an Australian car and _____ Alice Springs, _____
_____. He will soon visit Darwin. From there, he will fly
to Perth. My brother has never _____ before, so he is
finding this trip very _____.

*Supposing you are the author's brother, what will he say after
coming back from the trip.*

Ⅳ Active questions

1. What have you just received?
2. Who was it from?
3. Where was your brother from?
4. What does he do?
5. Has he visited many places in Australia?
6. What car has he just bought?
7. Where has he gone?
8. Is Alice Springs a small town or a big town?
9. How will he go to Perch?
10. Is he enjoying his trip very much? Why?

5

No wrong numbers
无错号之虞

I Use the word (s) to make sentence (s)

Telephone

_____.

Telephone — number

_____.

Telephone — number — message

_____.

Request

_____.

Request — her

_____.

Request — her — sent

_____.

Garage

_____.

Garage — cover

_____.

Garage — cover — second

_____.

II Practice the key patterns

T: 500 meters — from — to

S1: How far is from your home to your school?

S2: It is only 500 meters from my home to my school.

S3: My home is only 500 meters from my school.

Practice: (1) 1000 kilometers long

(2) ten kilometers away

(3) ten minutes walk

(4) 100 feet

T: write a letter to my mother — last week

S1: Have you written your mother a letter?

S2: Yes, I have. I wrote her a letter last week.

Practice: (1) receive a birthday cake — yesterday

(2) go to England — last month

(3) buy a sports car — last month

(4) have supper — an hour ago

(5) finish the task — two days ago

T: go to America — last month — two weeks

S1: When did you go to American?

S2: I went to America last month.

S1: How long were you there?

S2: I was there for two weeks.

Practice: (1) go abroad — in 2000 — seven years

(2) go to Hainan — last year — one year

(3) on business — ten days ago — a month

(4) go to the remote village — last November — a year

(5) go to visit Chengdu — last summer — fifteen days

T: cover — snow

S1: The ground will be covered with snow.

S2: Will the ground be covered with snow?

Practice: (1) fill — water

(2) make — wood

(3) staff — picture

(4) cover — sand

III Retell the story

Firstly complete the blanks and remember what you said.

Mr. James Scott has a garage in Silbury and now he _____

_____ in Pinhurst. Pinhurst is only five miles _____

Silbury, but Mr. Scott cannot _____ for his new garage,

so he has just bought twelve pigeons. Yesterday, a pigeon carried the

first _____ from Pinhurst to Silbury. The bird covered _____

_____ in three minutes. _____, Mr. Scott has sent a

great many requests for _____ and other urgent messages

from one garage to the other. In this way, he has begun his own

private " _____."

Secondly retell the story in the third person.

IV Active questions

Answer these questions in not more than 50 words.

回答下列问题，不要超过 50 个单词。

1. Where has Mr. Scott opened his second garage?

2. Where is his first garage?

3. How far away is Silbury?

4. Can Mr. Scott get a telephone for his new garage or not?

5. What has he bought?

6. In how many minutes do they carry messages from one garage
   to the other?

Lesson 6

Percy Buttons
珀西·巴顿斯

I Use the word (s) to make sentence (s)

Ask

_____

Ask — beggar

_____

Ask — beggar — about

_____

Call at

_____

Call at — twice

_____

Call at — twice — a week

_____

Knock at

_____

Knock at — beer

_____

Knock at — beer — house

_____

II Practice the key patterns

T: have lunch — before — finish

S1: Will the girl have lunch before she finishes her homework?

S2: The girl even won't have lunch before she finishes her homework.

Practice: (1) visit the chemical factory — after — have breakfast

(2) mend the bike — before — go out

(3) wash the dishes — until — come back

(4) know her — before — happen

T: call — once a month

S1: How often do you call your parents?

S2: Once a month.

(1) visit — three times a week

(2) call at — twice a day

(3) go to — three times a year

(4) receive an offer — never

T: a bar of soap

S1: I need a bar of soap.

S2: I've got some. I can lend it to you.

S1: No, thanks. I want to buy some.

(1) a bar of chocolate

(2) a cup of coffee

(3) a can of petrol

(4) a piece of chalk

(5) a bag of sugar

(6) a loaf of bread

III Retell the story

Firstly complete the blanks and remember what you said.

I have just _____ a house in Bridge Street. Yesterday

a beggar _____ my door. He asked me for a meal and a glass of beer. _____ , the beggar stood on his head and sang songs. I gave him a meal. He _____ the food and _____ the beer. Then he put a piece of cheese in his pocket and _____ _____ . Later a neighbor told me _____ him. Everybody knows him. His name is Percy Buttons. He _____ every house in the street once a month and _____ .

Secondly retell the story in the third person.

Ⅳ Active questions

1. Who is Percy Buttons in the text?
2. Where did you move?
3. Who knocked at your door yesterday?
4. What did he want to do?
5. What did he do in return for this?
6. Is everybody in the street familiar with him?
7. What is the beggar's name?
8. How often does he call at every house in the street?

Lesson 7

Too late

为时太晚

I Use the word (s) to make sentence (s)

Detective

_____.

Detective — spy on

_____.

Detective — spy on — airfield

_____.

Surprise

_____.

Surprise — steal

_____.

Surprise — steal — gold

_____.

Weekend

_____.

Weekend — buy

_____.

Weekend — buy — jeans

_____.

II Practice the key patterns

T: arrived — begging

S1: What was he doing when the police arrived?

S2: He was begging on the street when the police arrived.

Practice: (1) came in — drawing

(2) knocked at — sleeping

(3) visited — doing my homework

(4) came — having breakfast

(5) rang — reading the newspaper

(6) went out — working in the lab

T: make some dumplings — since — cook

S: We have made some dumplings since we began to cook.

Practice: (1) see each other — since — part

(2) six years — since — graduate

(3) stay here — until — come back

(4) clean the car — while — play the computer games

T: to one's surprise

S: To my surprise, he failed in the exam.

Practice: (1) to one's satisfaction

(2) to one's joy

(3) to one's advantage

(4) to one's sorrow

III Retell the story

Firstly complete the blanks and remember what you said.

The plane was late and detectives were waiting _____

all morning. They were expecting a valuable parcel of _____

from South Africa. A few hours earlier, someone had told the police that _____ . _____ , some of the detectives were waiting inside the main building while others were waiting on the airfield.

Two men took the parcel off the plane and _____ the Customs House. While two detectives were _____ at the door, two others opened the parcel. To their surprise, the precious parcel was full of _____ !

Secondly retell the story in the third person.

IV Active questions

1. How long were detectives waiting at the airport?
2. What were they expecting from South Africa?
3. Where did two men take the parcel after the arrival of the plane?
4. What had happened a few hours earlier?
5. How many detectives opened it?
6. Who were keeping guard at the door?
7. What was the parcel full of?

Lesson 8

The best and the worst
最好的和最差的

I Use the word (s) to make sentence (s)

Some

_____.

Some — more

_____.

Some — more — the most

_____.

Sweet

_____.

Sweet — sweeter

_____.

Sweet — sweeter — sweetest

_____.

Fast

_____.

Fast — faster

_____.

Fast — faster — fastest

_____.

II Practice the key patterns

T: Kate — Andy — Layton — fat — fatter — the fattest one in the class

S1: Kate is fat, but Andy is fatter than Kate.

S2: Layton is fatter than Andy. He is the fattest boy in the class.

Practice: (1) Tom — Jane — Peter — tall — taller — the tallest of all

(2) Tim's picture — Susan's picture — Xiao Hua's picture — beautiful — more beautiful — the most beautiful in the picture show

(3) volleyball — basketball — football — popular — more popular — the most popular

(4) I — my father — my mother — busy — busier — the busiest in the family

T: my computer — as dear as — yours

S1: My computer is more dear than yours.

S2: No, your computer is as dear as mine.

Practice: (1) the cars made in the U. S. A. — as good as — the cars made in Japan

(2) Kate — as tall as — Dickens

(3) Li Ming — as clever as — any other in the class

(4) the temperature today — as high as — the temperature yesterday

(5) the math exam — as hard as — the English exam

T: his lecture — interesting — heard

S1: What do you think of his lecture?

S2: It is the most interesting lecture I've ever heard.

Practice: (1) the computer game — dull — played

(2) last week's concert — wonderful — watched

（3）report — important — listened

（4）this trip — interesting — been to

（5）the plants — flourish — seen

Ⅲ Retell the story

Firstly complete the blanks and remember what you said.

Joe Sanders has the ＿＿＿＿＿＿＿＿ garden in our town. Nearly everybody enters for 'The Nicest Garden Competition' each year, but ＿＿＿＿＿＿＿＿. Bill Frith's garden is ＿＿＿＿ than Joe's. Bill works harder than Joe and grows ＿＿＿＿ flowers and vegetables, but Joe's garden is more interesting. He has ＿＿＿＿ ＿＿ and has built ＿＿＿＿＿＿＿＿ over a pool. I like gardens too, but I do not like hard work. Every year I enter for the garden ＿＿＿＿ too, and I always win a little prize for the ＿＿＿ ＿＿＿＿ in the town!

Secondly retell the story in the third person.

Ⅳ Active questions

1. Who has the most beautiful garden in the town?

2. Does everybody enter for 'The Nicest Garden Competition' each year?

3. Who wins each time?

4. Why is it?

5. Who else had a pretty good garden? Is his larger than Joe's?

6. Whose garden grows more flowers and vegetables?

7. Where has Bill Frith built a wooden bridge?

8. Whose garden is the worst in the town?

V Complete the sentences in the correct form

1. Shanghai is _____ industrial center in China. (big)

2. The film shown today is much _____ the one shown yesterday! (interest)

3. This is _____ book that I have ever read. (excite)

4. As the car was running _____ and _____, I told him to drive _____. (fast; careful)

5. Of all the hospitals in Shanghai, Zhongshan Hospital has got _____ doctors. (many)

6. Of all the girl students in Grade 1, Susan studies _____. (hard)

7. The car is running far _____ it used to. (smooth)

8. Can we do the work with _____ money and people to save the cost? (little; few)

9. Can you show me _____ book at the moment? (popular)

10. English is _____ Chinese. So we should learn both subjects well. (importance)

Lesson 9

A cold welcome

I *Use the word (s) to make sentence (s)*

Foot

_____.

Foot — strike

_____.

Foot — strike — stone

_____.

Friday

_____.

Friday — gather

_____.

Friday — gather — tower

_____.

Clock

_____.

Clock — move

_____.

Clock — move — hand

_____.

II Practice the key patterns

T: Friday — gather — in the hall

S1: When did a crowd of people gather in the hall?

S2: It was Friday and a crowd of people gathered in the hall.

Practice: (1) last day — meet — at school

(2) Christmas Eve — celebrate — on the street

(3) first day — buy — in the supermarket

(4) Monday — open — in Beijing

(5) an important day — the Olympic Games — in Beijing

T: 12:30 — twelve thirty — half past twelve

S1: What time is it?

S2: It is 12:30 (twelve thirty).

S3: It is half past twelve.

Practice: (1) 1:50

(2) 2:30

(3) 10:05

(4) 9:46

(5) 7:00

(6) 8:10

T: wait — but — happen

S: He waited and waited but nothing happened.

Practice: (1) knock at — although — be afraid

(2) be late — but — visit his grandfather

(3) sing and dance — while — play the violin

(4) collect coins — and — paint

(5) pass the exam — however — stop

III Retell the story

Firstly complete the blanks and remember what you said.

On Wednesday evening, we went to the Town Hall. It was ____ _____ and a large crowd of people had _____ under the Town Hall clock. It would _____ twelve in twenty minutes' time. Fifteen minutes passed and then, _____, the clock stopped. _____ did not move. We waited and waited, but _____ happened. Suddenly someone shouted. 'I _____' I looked at my watch. It was true. The big clock refused to welcome _____. At that moment, everybody began to _____ and _____.

Secondly retell the story in the third person.

IV Active questions

1. Where did you go on Wednesday evening?
2. What was the date?
3. Where did the crowd of people gather?
4. When would the Town Hall clock strike twelve?
5. At what time did the clock stop?
6. Which hand did not move?
7. What happened then?
8. What did someone shout suddenly?
9. What did you do after hearing it?
10. What time was it by your watch?
11. Did the big clock refuse to welcome the New Year?
12. What did everyone begin to do at that moment?

Lesson 10

Not for jazz
不适于演奏爵士乐

I Use the word(s) to make sentence(s)

New

_____

New — piano

_____

New — piano — buy

_____

String

_____

String — break

_____

String — break — yesterday

_____

Happen

_____

Happen — give

_____

Happen — give — shock

_____

II Practice the key patterns

T: musical instrument — bought — my grandfather

S1: Who bought the musical instrument?

S2: My grandfather bought the musical instrument.

S3: Who bought the musical instrument?

S4: It was bought by my grandfather.

Practice: (1) road — built — a famous engineer

(2) dynamite — invented — Nobel

(3) electricity — discovered — Benjamin Franklin

(4) book — wrote — John

(5) picture — drew — a skillful artist

(6) room — decorated — an experienced designer

T: allow — to smoke

S1: You are allowed to smoke here.

S2: They allowed you to smoke here.

Practice: (1) allow — to enter

(2) permit — to play piano

(3) tell — to work hard

(4) ask — to translate this paragraph

T: the project — finished

S1: Has the project been finished yet?

S2: Yes, it finished three months ago.

S3: Not yet.

Practice: (1) the room — cleaned

(2) the railway — completed

(3) the film — produced

(4) the clothes — washed

III Retell the story

Firstly complete the blanks and remember what you said.

We have an old musical _____. It is called a _____. It was made in Germany in 1681. Our clavichord is _____ the living room. It has _____ our family for a long time. The instrument _____. Recently it was damaged by a visitor. She tried to play jazz on it! She _____ too hard and two of the strings _____. My father was _____. Now we are not _____ it. It is being _____ by a friend of my father's.

Secondly retell the story in the third person.

IV Active questions

1. What is the name of our old music instrument?
2. Where was it made?
3. Where is the clavichord kept now?
4. Whose is it?
5. When was the instrument bought by my grandfather?
6. What happened to it recently?
7. What did the visitor do to the instrument?
8. How did she strike the keys?
9. What did she break?
10. Was my father shocked?
11. Who is repairing it?

Lesson 11

One good turn deserves another 礼尚往来

I Use the word (s) to make sentence (s)

Dinner

_____.

Dinner — restaurant

_____.

Have — dinner — restaurant

_____.

Work

_____.

Work — bank

_____.

Work — bank — now

_____.

Deserve

_____.

Deserve — praise

_____.

Deserve — praise — last week

_____.

II Practice the key patterns

T: he — work at a bank — this year

S1: What is he doing this year?

S2: He is working at a bank this year.

S3: Where is he working this year?

S4: He is working at a bank this year.

S5: When is he working at a bank?

S6: This year he is working at a bank.

Practice: (1) she — study English — at the moment

(2) they — play a game — right now

(3) his brother — fly a kite — now

(4) my cousin — ride a bike — at the present

T: Susan — watch a volleyball game on TV — last week

S1: What did Susan do last week?

S2: Susan watched a volleyball game on TV last week.

S3: When did Susan watch a Volleyball game?

S4: Last week.

S5: How did Susan watch a volleyball game?

S6: Susan watched a volleyball game on TV.

Practice: (1) she — read a novel at home — last month

(2) their family — visit their grandparents — yesterday

(3) the travelers — arrive at the station — at seven yesterday

(4) two classmates — have a quarrel — the day before yesterday

T: I — having dinner at a restaurant — Tony came in

S1: What was I doing when Tony came in?

S2: I was having dinner when Tony came in.

S3: What happened when I was having dinner?

S4: Tony came in when I was having dinner.

S5: Where was I having dinner when Tony came in?

S6: I was having dinner at a restaurant when Tony came in.

Practice: (1) I — reading a book in the lab — Jim rushed into my room

(2) Lisa — cleaning the floor in the classroom — Mom opened the door

(3) they — watching TV at home — she dropped the magazine

(4) he — repairing the chair in the garden — his sister turned on the radio

III Retell the story

Firstly complete the blanks and remember what you said.

I was _____ at a restaurant when Tony Steele came in. Tony worked in a _____ 's office years ago, but he is now _____. He gets a good _____, but he always borrows money from his friends and never _____. Tony saw me and came and sat at the same table. He has never borrowed money from me. While he was eating, I _____ pounds. To my surprise, he _____ immediately. ' I have never borrowed any money from you,' Tony said, ' so now you can ____ _____ my dinner!'

Secondly retell the story in the third person.

IV Active questions

1. Where were you having dinner?
2. Did Tony once work in a lawyer's office?
3. What does he do now?

4. What does he always do?
5. Has he ever borrowed money from you?
6. What did you do while he was eating?
7. Were you surprised?
8. What did he give you immediately?
9. What did he say?
10. At last who paid for the dinner?

Lesson 12

Goodbye and good luck
再见，一路顺风

I Use the word(s) to make sentence(s)

Take

_____.

Take — pride

_____.

Take — pride — in

_____.

Take

_____.

Take — part

_____.

Take — part — in

_____.

Telephone

_____.

Telephone — tell

_____.

Telephone — tell — out

_____.

II Practice the key patterns

T: see my aunt — tomorrow

S1: What will you do tomorrow?

S2: I will see my aunt tomorrow.

Practice: (1) return — in two minutes

(2) leave very early — tomorrow morning

(3) be absent from home — for two months

(4) start his journey — at 8 o'clock

(5) be at the airport — at 9: 50

(6) go to work — next week

T: go for the beach — tomorrow

S1: Shall we go for the beach tomorrow?

S2: Good idea.

S1: When shall we go for the beach?

S2: Tomorrow.

Practice: (1) meet at the school gate — the day after tomorrow

(2) play football — this afternoon

(3) go to the National Park — next week

(4) write an application letter to IBM — on Monday

(5) read in the library — later

T: go shopping — tomorrow — go to see my aunt

S1: We're going shopping tomorrow. Will you go with us?

S2: Sorry, I'm going to see my aunt tomorrow.

(1) go skating — next Sunday — on business

(2) go fishing — next weekend — go swimming

(3) go to the cinema — tomorrow afternoon — do my homework

(4) have a meeting — next Friday — meet a client

III Retell the story

Firstly complete the blanks and remember what you said.

Our neighbor, Captain Charles Alison, will _____ from Portsmouth tomorrow. We'll meet him at the _____ early in the morning. He will be _____, Topsail. Topsail is _____. It has sailed _____ the Atlantic many times. Captain Alison will _____ at eight o'clock, so we'll have _____. We'll _____ and then we'll _____ him. He will be away for two months. We are very _____ him. He will _____ an important race _____ the Atlantic.

Secondly retell the story in the third person.

IV Active questions

Answer these questions in not more than 45 words.

回答下列问题，不要超过45个单词。

1. Whom shall we meet at Portsmouth Harbour early tomorrow moming?
2. Where will he be?
3. At what time will he leave?
4. Shall we say goodbye to him, or shall we travel with him?
5. What will he take part in?

Lesson 13

The Greenwood Boys
绿林少年

I Use the word (s) to make sentence (s)

A group of

_____.

A group of — islands

_____.

A group of — islands — lake

_____

Prefer

_____.

Prefer — popular

_____.

Prefer — popular — rock

_____

Performance

_____.

Performance — maths

_____.

Performance — maths — good

_____.

II Practice the key patterns

T: flying to Guangzhou — at 8 tomorrow morning

S1: What will you be doing at 8 tomorrow morning?

S2: At that time I will be flying to Guangzhou.

Practice: (1) watching television — all day and all night

(2) taking my holiday — soon

(3) having tea — after lunch as usual

(4) have a meeting — at 9 tomorrow morning

T: leave — 10 o'clock

S1: What time is the next plane to Boston?

S2: It leaves at 10 o'clock.

Practice: (1) come — this morning

(2) start — tomorrow

(3) stay — all day

(4) get — next month

T: delicious — food

S1: How is the food like?

S2: What delicious food it is!

S3: How delicious the food is!

Practice: (1) interesting — film

(2) cold — weather

(3) happy — they

(4) clever — boy

(5) nice — watch

(6) tall — tree

III Retell the story

Firstly complete the blanks and remember what you said.

The Greenwood Boys are a group of _____ singers. At

present, they are visiting all parts of the country. They will be arriving here tomorrow. They will _____ and most of the young people in the town will be meeting them _____. Tomorrow evening they will _____ at the Workers' Club. The Greenwood Boys will _____. During this time, they will give five performances. As usual, the police will have a _____ _____ time. They will be trying to _____. It is always the same _____.

Secondly retell the story in the third person.

IV Active questions

1. Who are the Greenwood Boys?
2. Are they famous in the town?
3. Where are they going to visit at present?
4. When will they arrive here?
5. Where will they be singing tomorrow evening?
6. How many performances will they have?
7. Why will the police have a different time?
8. Does it often happen in this town?

Do you speak English?
你会讲英语吗?

I Use the word(s) to make sentence(s)

Ask

_____ .

Ask — reply

_____ .

Ask — reply — English

_____ .

Journey

_____ .

Journey — enjoy

_____ .

Journey — enjoy — during

_____ .

Exciting

_____ .

Exciting — travel

_____ .

Exciting — travel — experience

_____ .

II Practice the key patterns

T: leave — as soon as — hear the news

S: He left as soon as he heard the news.

Practice: (1) call you — when — come back

(2) draw the picture — while — come in

(3) write to me — as soon as — finish the work

(4) tell him the truth — as soon as — arrive

T: had left — arrived

S: Most of the guests had left when he arrived at the party.

Practice: (1) had been away — arrived

(2) had died — flew home

(3) had done his homework — went out to play football

(4) had got to the station — left

(5) had planned this project — provided

T: learned that song — was in Shanghai

S1: When did you learn that song?

S2: I learned that song when I was in Shanghai last month.

Practice: (1) moved here — 10 years old

(2) were at dinner — went to see them

(3) listen to the pop music — was a child

(4) met my best friend — took my journey

III Retell the story

Firstly complete the blanks and remember what you said.

I had _____ last year. After I had left a _____

_____ in the south of France, I _____ to the next

town. On the way, a young man _____ to me. I _____

_____. As soon as he had got into the car, I said _____

_____ to him in French and he replied in the _____
language. Apart from a few words, I do not know _____
____ at all. Neither of us spoke during the journey. I had nearly
reached the town, when the young man suddenly said, very slowly,
_____? ' As I soon learnt, he was English
himself! '

Secondly retell the story in the third person.

Ⅳ Active questions

1. When did you have such an amusing experience?

2. What did you do after you had left a small village?

3. Why did the young man wave to you?

4. What did he want me to do?

5. Did you agree?

6. What did you say when he had got into the car?

7. Did they greet each other in French?

8. Did you speak any French except a few words?

9. What did you speak in the car?

10. What did the man ask me when he was ready to get off the car?

11. What did you learn from his words?

Lesson

15   Good news

住音

I Use the word (s) to make sentence (s)

Feel

_____

Feel — disappointed

_____

Feel — disappointed — fail

_____.

Can't

_____.

Can't — afford

_____.

Can't — afford — villa

_____.

Pay

_____.

Pay — extra

_____.

Pay — extra — fee

_____.

II Practice the key patterns

T: Open your books.

S1: What did he say?

S2: He told us to open our books.

Practice: (1) close the door

(2) come this way, please

(3) don't touch this bottle

(4) turn left and go straight

(5) come for dinner together

(6) speak English more often in and out of class

T: He said, 'I get on well with the people here.'

S1: What did he say?

S2: He said that he got on well with the people there.

Practice: (1) Susan said, 'We can finish the work tomorrow.'

(2) John said to me, 'I told her all about it three days ago.'

(3) He said, 'I like swimming and I want to go swimming with you.'

(4) She said, 'I don't fell very well.'

T: Will you be back today?

S1: What did the teacher ask?

S2: The teacher asked (him) if / whether he would be back that day.

Practice: (1) He asked, 'Has the bell rung?'

(2) 'Shall (Should) I tell her your telephone number?' he asked me.

(3) 'Would you like to help me with my lessons?' she asked me.

(4) He asked, 'Who can carry the box?'

(5) He asked, 'Who is the man near the window?'

(6) 'Which one do you like best here?' he asked her.

(7) 'How shall (should) I read the book?' she asked.

III Retell the story

Firstly complete the blanks and remember what you said.

The secretary told me that Mr. Harmsworth would see me. I felt very _____ when I went into his office. He did not _____ _____ when I entered. After I had sat down, he said that _____ _____. He told me that _____ _____. Twenty people had already left. I knew that my turn had come.

'Mr. Harmsworth,' I said in a weak voice.

'Don't _____,' he said.

Then he smiled and told me I would receive _____ _____ _____!

Secondly retell the story in the third person.

IV Active questions

1. Who is Mr. Harmsworth?

2. What did the secretary tell me?

3. Where did you go?

4. How did you feel at that time?

5. What did he talk to me after I had sat down?

6. What did he say about business?

7. What did he tell you?

8. How many people had already left?

9. What did you think at the time?

10. How did you speak to him?

11. Did he ask you to leave as well?

Lesson 16

A polite request
彬彬有礼的要求

I Use the word(s) to make sentence(s)

Park

_____.

Park — traffic

_____.

Park — traffic — jam

_____.

Area

_____.

Area — ticket

_____.

Area — ticket — prohibit

_____.

Obey

_____.

Obey — law

_____.

Obey — law — citizen

_____.

II Practice the key patterns

T: park — the policeman — find

S1: What will happen if you park your car in the wrong place?

S2: If I park my car in the wrong place, the policeman will find it.

S3: The policeman will find my car if I park it in the wrong place.

Practice: (1) not pay attention to — the cup — break

(2) eat bad food — you — are ill

(3) have time — we — go hiking together

(4) break the law — you — be punished

(5) catch the bus — they — be on time

(6) make a journey — you — see many spots

T: he is young — he knows

S: Although he is young, he knows a lot of things.

Practice: (1) they don't like — they accept

(2) she is fat — she continues keeping fit

(3) he works hard — he has no chance to...

(4) Lucy concentrates in class — she can't catch...

T: hurry up — catch the train

S1: Hurry up or you won't catch the train.

S2: If you don't hurry up, you will miss the train.

Practice: (1) work hard — pass the exam

(2) give up the smoke — be healthy

(3) speak loudly — hear

(4) obey the rules — be punished

III Retell the story

Firstly complete the blanks and remember what you said.

If you _____ your car in the wrong place, a traffic policeman

will soon find it. You will be very lucky if _____ .
However, this does not always happen. Traffic police are sometimes
very _____ . During a holiday in Sweden, I found this _____
on my car: 'sir, we welcome you to our city. _____ .
You will enjoy your stay here if you _____ our
street signs. This note is only a _____ . ' If you receive a request
like this, you cannot fail to _____ it!

Secondly retell the story in the third person.

Ⅳ Active questions

1. What will happen if you park the car in the wrong place?
2. Will the policeman let you go if you park the car in the wrong
   place?
3. Does it always happen?
4. Are the traffic police always polite?
5. Where did you find a note on your car?
6. What did the note say?
7. Why did the police leave a note on your car?
8. What do you think of this note?
9. The note was only a reminder, wasn't it?
10. Can anyone fail to obey a request like this?

Ⅴ Translation

1. He told us that he felt ill.
2. I know he has returned.
3. I am not sure what I ought to do.
4. I'm afraid you don't understand what I said.
5. We can walk there if we can't find a bus.

6. If it rains tomorrow, we will not go to the zoo.

7. What will you do if you find a panda in danger.

8. I feel very happy when you come to see me.

9. When you are crossing the street, you must be careful.

10. If I get there early, I can see the doctor quickly.

Lesson 17

Always young

青春常驻

Act

_____.

Act — actor

_____.

Act — actor — actress

_____.

Take part in

_____.

Take part in — party

_____.

Take part in — party — recently

_____.

Dress

_____.

Dress — wear

_____.

Dress — wear — stockings

_____.

· 53 ·

II Practice the key patterns

T: young — you must excuse him

S1: Why did you excuse him?

S2: He was so young that you must excuse him.

Practice: (1) pinch so well — everybody cheered him

(2) fat — he didn't catch up with the other students

(3) fierce — nobody dares to touch it

(4) tired — they could do nothing but yawn

(5) dark — I couldn't see it

(6) tired — she went to bed early

T: story book — Kate's — read it

S1: Is this book yours?

S2: No, it is not mine. It must be Kate's.

S1: How do you know?

S2: I saw him reading it yesterday.

Practice: (1) house — Mr. Smith's — move the furniture

(2) car — Susan's — drive it

(3) pencil — Xiao Ming's — use it

(4) shirt — my brother — wear it

T: finish everything tonight

S1: Must I finish everything tonight?

S2: Yes, you must.

S3: No, you needn't. You may finish it tomorrow.

Practice: (1) leave early

(2) remember all the English words today

(3) be off now

(4) take the medicine twice a day

(5) come tonight

(6) come round tonight

Ⅲ Retell the story

Firstly complete the blanks and remember what you said.

My aunt Jennifer is _____. She must be _____
thirty-five years old. In spite of this, she often _____
____. Jennifer will have to take part in a new V soon. This time, she
will be a girl of seventeen. In the play, she must appear in _____
_____. Last year in another play, she had to _____
_____. If anyone ever asks her _____, she
always answers, 'Darling, it must be terrible to be _____!'
Secondly retell the story in the third person.

Ⅳ Active questions

1. What does Jennifer do?
2. How old is she actually?
3. What role does she often play on the stage?
4. Will she have a new play soon?
5. Is she playing a girl of seventeen?
6. In the play, what clothes must she wear?
7. What color is her dress in another play last year?
8. If anyone asks her age, how does she answer?

Lesson 18

He often does this!
他经常干这种事！

I Use the word(s) to make sentence(s)

Lunch

_____.

Lunch — village pub

_____.

Lunch — village pub — chat

_____.

Leave

_____.

Leave — door

_____.

Leave — door — beside

_____.

Landlord

_____.

Landlord — bill

_____.

Landlord — bill — reply

_____.

II　Practice the key patterns

T:　a dictionary

S1:　Have you got a dictionary?

S2:　Yes, I have.

S3:　Do you have a dictionary?

S4:　Yes, I do.

Practice:　（1）something to tell you

　　　　　（2）a headache

　　　　　（3）a lot of money

　　　　　（4）a pen

T:　smile — go out

S:　The landlord smiled and then went out.

Practice:　（1）drink the tea — come in

　　　　　（2）return with my bag — give it back to me

　　　　　（3）get up — dress herself

　　　　　（4）come to the decision — act at once

T:　give it to Susan

S1:　Have you given it to Susan yet?

S2:　Yes, I have. I gave it to Susan last night.

S3:　No, I have not. I will give it to Susan tomorrow.

Practice:　（1）buy the fruit in the supermarket

　　　　　（2）see her this afternoon

　　　　　（3）write some short stories

　　　　　（4）ring up three times

　　　　　（5）make a cake

　　　　　（6）paint the picture

　　　　　（7）built a bridge between the two cities

　　　　　（8）know each for a long time

III Retell the story

Firstly complete the blanks and remember what you said.

After I had had lunch at a _____, I _____. I
had left it on a chair beside the door and now _____! As I
was looking for it, the landlord came in.

'Did you have a good _____?' he asked.

'Yes, thank you,' I answered, 'but I can't _____. I
haven't got my bag.'

The landlord _____ and immediately _____. _____
_____ he returned with my bag and _____ it _____ to me.

'I'm very sorry,' he said. 'My dog had _____
____. He often does this!'

Secondly retell the story in the third person.

IV Active questions

1. Where have you had lunch?

2. What did you do afterwards?

3. Where did you leave your bag?

4. Was it still there?

5. What did the landlord ask me when he came in?

6. What was your reply?

7. What did he do?

8. What did he bring back?

9. Was he sorry for that?

10. Where had the dog taken it?

11. Does the dog often do this?

V Translation

1. 你在找什么?

2. 我找不到我的鞋子。

3. 我一直在找地图，找了半个小时终于找着了。
4. 他在门上留了一张条子。
5. 我想我一定是把钥匙留在屋里了。
6. 他带来了坏消息。
7. 他带着雨伞出去了。
8. have a cigarette
9. have a holiday
10. have a rest

Sold out

票已售完

I Use the word (s) to make sentence (s)

Hurry

_____ .

Hurry — office

_____ .

Hurry — office — sad

_____ .

Return

_____ .

Return — ticket

_____ .

Return — ticket — gladly

_____ .

Pity

_____ .

Pity — steal

_____ .

Pity — steal — bicycle

_____ .

Ⅱ Practice the key patterns

T: come — watch TV

S1: Did he come yesterday?

S2: No, he didn't come. He must have watched TV at home.

S3: No, he didn't come. He may have watched TV at home, but I'm not sure.

S4: No, he didn't come. He might have watched TV at home, but I'm not sure.

Practice: (1) be out — telephone the police office

(2) come back home — overdrink

(3) be in the classroom — have a discussion

(4) have breakfast — run in the playground

(5) use your computer — repair his computer

T: prove it

S1: Can you prove it?

S2: Yes, of course.

Practice: (1) borrow your pencil

(2) overcome the difficulty

(3) call for her at nine

(4) follow me

(5) lend me your car

(6) come round in the morning

T: look up — the dictionary

S1: May I look up the words in the dictionary?

S2: He asked me if he might look up the words in the dictionary.

Practice: (1) finish everything in time

(2) leave more later

(3) trouble you for a moment

(4) use your mobile phone

（5）go shopping at this time

（6）have your signature on the bottom of the paper

Ⅲ Retell the story

Firstly complete the blanks and remember what you said.

'The play may _____ at any moment,' I said.

'_____,' Susan answered.

I _____ the ticket office. 'May I have two tickets please?' I asked.

'I'm sorry, we've _____,' the girl said.

'_____ !' Susan exclaimed.

Just then, a man _____.

'Can I _____ these two tickets?' he asked.

'Certainly,' the girl said.

I went back to the ticket office at once.

'_____?' I asked.

'Certainly,' the girl said, 'but they're for next Wednesday's __
_____. Do you still want them?'

'I _____ have them,' I said sadly.

Secondly retell the story in the third person.

Ⅳ Active questions

1. When was the play going to begin?

2. Whom was I talking to?

3. What did you plan to do?

4. How many tickets did you want?

5. What did the girl answer?

6. Were there any left?

7. Were you glad to hear that?

8. Who hurried to the ticket wicket just then?
9. What did he want to do?
10. When was the performance?
11. Did you decide to buy the tickets?

Lesson 20

One man in a boat

独坐孤舟

I Use the word (s) to make sentence (s)

Fish

_____.

Fish — catch

_____.

Fish — catch — fisherman

_____.

School

_____.

School — instead of

_____.

School — instead of — home

_____.

Empty

_____.

Empty — bag

_____.

Empty — bag — disappointed

_____.

II Practice the key patterns

T: fishing — sport

S1: What is your favorite sport?

S2: Fishing is my favorite sport.

S3: My favorite sport is fishing.

Practice:　(1) eating — pleasure

　　　　　(2) watching TV — pastime

　　　　　(3) reading in bed — enjoy

　　　　　(4) walking on the street — romantic thing

　　　　　(5) spending on the river — waste of time

T: she bought a pair of boots — (instead of) she did not get a pair of shoes

S1: She bought a pair of boots instead of getting a pair of shoes.

S2: She bought a pair of boots instead of a pair of shoes.

Practice:　(1) He went out of the restaurant. (without) He did not pay the bill.

　　　　　(2) They came back home. (without) They didn't get anything.

　　　　　(3) She was afraid. (of) She did not spend the night alone.

　　　　　(4) I am interested in reading English books. (instead of) I am not interested in reading math books.

　　　　　(5) I'm afraid I have to have dinner with them. (instead of) I have to shop with you tonight.

　　　　　(6) He congratulated me. (on) I won the competition.

　　　　　(7) I must apologize. (for) I did not let you know earlier.

　　　　　(8) He sat there. (without) He did not say anything.

T: he looked at this watch — he hurried to the station

S1: After looking at his watch, he hurried to the station.

S2: Before hurrying to the station, he looked at his watch.

Practice: (1) He turned off the radio. He left the room.

(2) She heard the sad news. She burst into tears.

(3) They gave me a lot of precious suggestions. I know how to deal with it.

(4) He heard the news. He fainted.

(5) I think carefully. I'll answer this question.

III Retell the story

Firstly complete the blanks and remember what you said.

Fishing is _____ . I often fish for hours _____ catching anything. But this does not _____ me. Some fishermen are unlucky. _____ , they catch old boots and rubbish. I am even _____ . I never catch anything — not even old boots. After having spent whole mornings on the river, _____ _____ . 'You must _____ fishing!' my friends say. 'It's _____ _____ .' But they don't realize one important thing. I'm not really interested in fishing. I am _____ !

Secondly retell the story in the third person.

IV Active questions

1. What is your favorite sport?

2. Do you often catch many fish?

3. Does this worry you?

4. Are you lucky in fishing?

5. Why are some fishermen unlucky?

6. What do you catch?

7. How long do you spend on the river?

8. What do you always go home with?

9. Do your friends encourage you?

10. What do they say?

11. Are you really interested in fishing?

12. What is the only thing that interests you?

Mad or not?
是不是疯了？

I Use the word (s) to make sentence (s) . . . .

Aeroplane

_____ .

Aeroplane — trouble

_____ .

Aeroplane — trouble — noise

_____ .

House

_____ .

House — knock down

_____ .

House — knock down — passing

_____ .

Determine

_____ .

Determine — stay

_____ .

Determine — stay — crazy

_____ .

Ⅱ Practice the key patterns

　　　　T: The passing plane will knock down this house.

S1: What does the man mean?

S2: He means that the passing plane will knock down this house.

S3: He means that this house will be knocked down by the passing plane.

Practice:（1）Dickens wrote his book.

　　　　　（2）They will announce the result until 6 o'clock.

　　　　　（3）He admitted me to come into the library.

　　　　　（4）They closed down the factory.

　　　　　（5）Susan invited me to his birthday party.

　　　　　（6）Mr. Smith praised me for what I have done.

　　　　　（7）My boss should send me to work abroad.

　　　　　（8）They will build the bridge next year.

　　　　T: produce her drama in July

S1: Do you know when her drama will be produced?

S2: I think her drama will be produced in July.

Practice:（1）finish the work next week

　　　　　（2）held the meeting tomorrow

　　　　　（3）break into the house at nine yesterday

　　　　　（4）send the applications by the end of September

　　　　　（5）publish the book next year

　　　　T: important — keep healthy

S1: It is important to keep healthy.

S2: Keeping healthy is important.

Practice:（1）interesting — go shopping with my sister

　　　　　（2）foolish — tell lies

　　　　　（3）essential — verify the truth

　　　　　（4）a good way — recite the text

(5) necessary — discuss the problem in the class

(6) right — help the poor people

(7) difficult — solve the problem

III Retell the story

Firstly complete the blanks and remember what you said.

Aeroplanes are slowly _____ . I live near an airport and passing planes can be _____ night and day. The airport was _____ years ago, but for some reason it could not _____ then. Last year, however, it _____ . Over a hundred people must have been _____ their homes by the noise. _____ _____ . Sometimes I think this house _____ by a passing plane. I have been offered _____ money to go away, but I _____ stay here. Everybody says I must be mad and they are _____ right.

Secondly retell the story in the third person.

IV Active questions

1. What makes me mad?
2. Where do you live?
3. When did the airport build?
4. When did it come to use?
5. Why have many people left their homes?
6. Did you determine to leave here?
7. What do you think sometimes?
8. What have you been offered if you left the home?
9. What are you determined to do?
10. What do people say about you?
11. Are they right to say so?

Lesson 22

A glass envelope
玻璃信封

I Use the word(s) to make sentence(s)

Dream

_____ .

Dream — sweet

_____ .

Dream — sweet — become

_____ .

Travel

_____ .

Travel — across

_____ .

Travel — across — Europe

_____ .

Paper

_____ .

Paper — address

_____ .

Paper — address — post office

_____ .

II Practice the key patterns

T: it is high time — go

S: It is high time we went.

Practice: (1) it is high time — leave

(2) it is high time — order dinner

(3) it is time — teach a lesson

(4) it is high time — buy a new car

(5) it is time — make up your mind

(6) it is time — get a new job and settle down

T: my niece — Maria

S1: Did you know who Maria is?

S2: She is my niece Maria.

Practice: (1) my aunt — Susan

(2) the Russian writer — Tolstoy

(3) our professor — Baker

(4) Beidaihe — a summer resort in Northern China

(5) six months — half the usual time

(6) Sophia — my best friend

T: English — is interested — math

S1: Do you know whether she is interested in English or not?

S2: No, she isn't interested in English. But I think she is interested in maths.

Practice: (1) swimming — prefer — skating

(2) IT industry — invest — consulting industry

(3) English exam — fail — physics exam

(4) his ability — pride — his action

III Retell the story

Firstly complete the blanks and remember what you said.

My daughter, Jane, never dreamed of _____

a girl of her own age in Holland. Last year, we were travelling _____

_____ the Channel and Jane put a piece of paper with her _____

_____ on it into a bottle. She _____ the bottle into the sea. She

never _____ it again, but ten months later, she _____

_____ from a girl in Holland. Both girls write to each other

_____ now. However, they have decided to use the _____

_____. Letters will _____ a little more, but they will certainly

_____.

Secondly retell the story in the third person.

IV Active questions

1. What is my daughter's name?

2. What did she never dream of?

3. When were you traveling across the Channel?

4. What did Jane do during the trip?

5. What was written on this piece of paper?

6. Where did she throw the bottle?

7. Did she think of it again?

8. What happened to her ten months later?

9. What do the two girls do regularly?

10. Why have they decided to use the post office to send the letters?

V Fill the blanks with the correct form of the verbs given

1. The children are singing in the room _____

（happy）

2. Look! We can go out for fun! The rain _____ .
   （stop）

3. Lesson 2 is _____ than Lesson 1. （difficult）

4. Don't forget _____ the door when you leave.
   （lock）

5. Jane is away on holidays. She _____ New York.
   （go）

6. I really enjoy _____ TV. （watch）

7. He usually _____ （go） to school on foot.

8. She always writes as _____ （care） as her teacher.

9. So far we _____ （have） no trouble.

10. The policy has made the _____ （business）
    excited.

Lesson
23

A new house

新居

I *Use the word (s) to make sentence (s)*

Complete

_____.

Complete — modern

_____.

Complete — modern — house

_____.

County

_____.

County — city

_____.

County — city — district

_____.

Strange

_____.

Strange — surprise

_____.

Strange — surprise — entire

_____.

II Practice the key patterns

T: She will come to England next year. (say)

S1: What did she say in her letter?

S2: She said that she would come to England next year.

Practice: (1) She has a strong will. (feel)

(2) They are against me. (know)

(3) He has arrived at the destination. (tell)

(4) All the children are well taken care of. (agree)

(5) You have won a scholarship. (hear)

(6) Everything goes well. (hope)

T: He explained, "I never eat meat."

S1: What did he explain?

S2: He explained that he never ate meat.

Practice: (1) "Who is it?" Wilson shouted.

(2) "We wish we didn't have to take exam," said the children.

(3) "I've already taken your son to the nursery," Jane said.

(4) "I bought these pearls for my mother," Joe said.

(5) She said to me, "You speak English better than me."

(6) He said, "I took it home with me."

(7) He said, "She is coming this week."

(8) He said, "This happened two years ago."

T: meeting a friend at Beijing airport next Monday

S1: Are you free next Monday? I want to talk about the lecture with you.

S2: Sorry, I'll be meeting a friend at Beijing airport next Monday.

S3: OK, no problem.

Practice: (1) having an interview tomorrow

（2）giving a presentation at nine tomorrow

（3）taking a math exam this afternoon

（4）build a shed at five the day after tomorrow

III Retell the story

Firstly complete the blanks and remember what you said.

I had a letter from my sister yesterday. She lives in _____.
In her letter, she said that _____. If
she comes, she will get a _____. We are now living in a beautiful
_____. Work on it had begun before _____.
The house was _____ five months ago. In my letter, I told her
that _____. The house has many large rooms and there
is a _____ garden. It is a very _____ house, so it looks
strange to some people. It must be the only modern house in the _____

_____.

Secondly retell the story in the third person.

IV Active questions

1. What did you receive from your sister?

2. Did she live in America?

3. What did she say in the letter?

4. Will she get a surprise if she comes?

5. Where are you living now?

6. When did the new house complete?

7. What did you tell her in your letter?

8. How many rooms do you have in your house?

9. Is there a beautiful garden?

10. What is the house like?

11. Is it the only modern house in the district?

Ⅴ Translation

1. I need three more words to complete the puzzle.

2. The house was completed five months ago.

3. He is crazy about modern art.

4. What strange clothes you're wearing!

5. This district of this country is famous for its vineyards and wine.

6. He asks me how many people there are in my family.

7. I have heard (that) he will come back next week.

8. I think English is very difficult to master.

9. Some people think it is easy to learn to play guitar.

10. He asked me if I know her telephone number.

Lesson 24

If could be worse
不幸中之万幸

I Use the word (s) to make sentence (s)

Promote

_____

Promote — manager

_____

Promote — manager — department

_____

Greatly

_____

Greatly — sympathetic

_____

Greatly — sympathetic — die

_____

Complain

_____

Complain — noise

_____

Complain — noise — corridor

_____

II Practice the key patterns

T: he started to complain about this wicked world —
was interrupted by a knock at the door

S: He started to complain about this wicked world but was interrupted by a knock at the door.

Practice: (1) they want to help him — they have no tool in hand

(2) the chocolate cake looks great — I have to watch my weight

(3) I wish I could — Japanese and of course English are the only languages I can speak

(4) Helen went to the store to buy some butter knives — she bought some soup spoons instead

T: my wife — buy a washing machine — her mother

S1: Who bought a washing machine?

S2: My wife bought a washing machine. I want to know whom she bought for?

S3: She bought it for her mother.

Practice: (1) the waiter — bring a cup of tea — the guest

(2) my sister — order some delicious dishes — me

(3) the doctor — prescribe some medicine — Susan

(4) my aunt — write a popular love story — her husband

(5) my best friend — prepare a rich dinner — me

(6) he — sing a song — her mother

T: She can swim like a fish.

S: She said she could swim like a fish.

Practice: (1) You may take it home.

(2) We'll support you.

(3) Shall I go with you?

(4) Should I shut the door?

(5) I oughtn't to do it.

(6) Could I take this seat?

(7) I must leave right now.

(8) You can finish it on time.

III Retell the story

Firstly complete the blanks and remember what you said.

I entered the hotel manager's office and ＿＿＿＿＿＿＿. I had just lost ＄50 and I felt very upset. 'I ＿＿＿＿＿＿＿ in my room,' I said, 'and it's not there now.' The manager was ＿＿＿＿, but he could do nothing. '＿＿＿＿＿＿＿＿＿＿＿＿,' he said. He started to ＿＿＿＿＿＿＿ this wicked world but was ＿＿＿＿＿＿＿. A girl came in and put an ＿＿＿＿ on his desk. It ＿＿＿＿＿ ＄50. 'I found this outside this gentleman's room,' she said. 'Well,' I said to the manager, '＿＿＿＿＿＿＿＿＿＿ !'

Secondly retell the story in the third person.

IV Active questions

1. Whose office did you go into?

2. What did you do?

3. How much did you lose?

4. Did you feel upset?

5. What did you say?

6. Could you find it?

7. Who was sympathetic?

8. What could he do to help you?

9. What did he say to you?

10. What did he begin to complain about?

11. What happened and then?
12. Who came into the office?
13. What did she put on the desk?
14. What did she say?
15. Where has she found it?
16. Is there still some honesty in this world?

Do the English speak English?

英国人讲的是英语吗?

I Use the word (s) to make sentence (s)

Railway

_____.

Railway — destroy

_____.

Railway — destroy — storm

_____.

Several

_____.

Several — concert

_____.

Several — concert — joy

_____.

Wonder

_____.

Wonder — if

_____.

Wonder — if — spare time

_____.

II Practice the key patterns

T: the post office

S1: Could you tell me the way to the post office?

S2: Where is the post office?

S3: How can I get to the post office?

Practice: (1) the nearest hospital

(2) Beijing Normal University

(3) the police station

(4) Modern plaza

(5) Chaoyang Park

(6) Tian'anmen square

T: I can speak Chinese. I can speak English.

S1: Can you speak Chinese?

S2: Yes, I can speak English as well.

S3: I can speak not only Chinese but also English.

Practice: (1) I can sing. I can dance.

(2) You will go there. I will go there.

(3) I like my mother. I like my father.

(4) You are not a good student. She is not a good student.

(5) Mary has gone abroad. Her parents have gone abroad.

(6) He is going to the airport. I am going to the airport.

T: Mary — Susan — does not like spicy food

S1: Mary doesn't like spicy food.

S2: Susan doesn't like spicy food, either.

S3: Neither does Susan.

S4: Nor does Susan.

S5: Neither Mary nor Susan likes spicy food.

Practice: (1) the red skirt — the green skirt — does not fit me

(2) I haven't read this book — that book on the shelf

（3）she — he — did not say anything

（4）this train — the next train — did not have a restaurant car

（5）what you said — what they said — is not right

III Retell the story

Firstly complete the blanks and remember what you said.

I _____ London at last. The railway station was big, black and dark. I did not know _____, so I asked a porter. I _____ spoke English very carefully, _____ very clearly _____. The porter, however, _____. I repeated my question _____ and at last he understood. he answered me, but _____. 'I am a foreigner,' I said. Then he spoke slowly, but I could not understand him. My teacher never _____! The porter and I looked at _____ and smiled. _____. 'You'll soon learn English!' he said. I wonder. In England, each person speaks a _____ language. The English understand each other, but I don't understand them! Do they speak English?

Secondly retell the story in the third person.

IV Active questions

Answer these questions in not more than 70 words.

回答下列问题，不要超过 70 个单词。

1. Did you arrive at a railway station in London or not? Did you ask a porter the way to your hotel or not? Could he understand you or not? (and... but)

2. Did he understand you at last or not? Could you understand his

answer? （but）

3. Did your teacher ever speak English like that or not?

4. What did the porter say to you?

5. Does each person speak a different language in England or not?

6. Do they understand each other or not? Do you understand them?
   （but）

Lesson
26

The best art critics
最佳艺术评论家

I Use the word (s) to make sentence (s)

Art

_____.

Art — modern

_____.

Art — modern — artist

_____.

Paint

_____.

Paint — critics

_____.

Paint — critics — appreciate

_____.

Notice

_____.

Notice — material

_____.

Notice — material — curtain

_____.

II Practice the key patterns

T: shopping at a supermarket — cheaper —
   going to the local shops

S1: Shopping at a supermarket is cheaper than going to the local shops.

S2: I don't agree with you. I think shopping at a supermarket is as cheap as going to the local shops.

Practice: (1) ski — more exciting — skate

(2) it — colder — yesterday

(3) I — fatter — my sister

(4) my sister — ten years younger — me

(5) this book — more useful — that one

(6) you look — happier — you did yesterday

T: Jim — tallest — any other students

S1: Jim is taller than any other students.

S2: Jim is the tallest in the class.

S3: Any other students are not so tall as Jim.

Practice: (1) he — kindest — I've ever met

(2) Changjiang — longest — in China

(3) the hospital — best — I've ever seen

(4) that — the most tasty meal — I've ever had

(5) this book — the most interesting — any other book

(6) jogging — in the playground

T: What is he doing?

S1: He is jogging in the playground.

S2: What does he like?

S3: He likes jogging. Look, he is jogging in the playground.

Practice: (1) swimming — in the pool

(2) listening to music — in his bedroom

(3) doing the housework — at home

(4) cooking — in the kitchen

(5) playing guitar — on the platform

(6) playing football — with his classmates

III Retell the story

Firstly complete the blanks and remember what you said.

I am an art and I paint ＿＿＿＿＿＿. Many people pretend that ＿＿＿＿＿＿＿＿＿＿＿＿. They always tell you what a picture is '＿＿＿＿＿'. Of course, many pictures are not 'about' anything. They are just pretty ＿＿＿＿. We like them ＿＿＿＿＿ ＿＿ that we like pretty curtain material. I think that ＿＿＿＿＿ ＿＿＿＿＿＿. They notice more. My sister is only seven, but she always tells me whether my pictures are good or not. She came into my room yesterday.

'What are you doing?' she asked.

'I'm ＿＿＿＿＿＿＿＿,' I answered. 'It's a new one. Do you like it?'

She looked at it ＿＿＿＿ for a moment. 'It's all right,' she said, 'but isn't it ＿＿＿＿＿＿?'

I looked at it again. She was right! It was!

Secondly retell the story in the third person.

IV Active questions

1. What do you do?

2. What do you paint?

3. What do many people pretend?

4. What do they always tell you?

5. Are many picture "about" anything?

6. In what way do we like pictures?

7. What pictures do the young children prefer?

8. How old is your sister?

9. What did she always tell you?

10. What did she do yesterday?

11. What did you do yesterday?

12. How did she look at the picture?

13. What did she notice?

14. Was she right or not?

Lesson 27

A wet night

雨夜

I Use the word(s) to make sentence(s)

Tent

_____ .

Tent — creep into

_____ .

Tent — creep into — wet

_____ .

Smoke

_____ .

Smoke — heavily

_____ .

Smoke — heavily — influence

_____ .

Smell

_____ .

Smell — campfire

_____ .

Smell — campfire — comfortable

_____ .

Ⅱ Practice the key patterns

T: Susan went to the trade fair.

S1: Do you know what Susan did yesterday?

S2: Sorry, I don't know. But I heard that she went to the trade fair.

Practice: (1) She joined a folk group and started singing.

(2) She went to play football.

(3) She went to the beach.

(4) They prepared for the exam.

(5) He lost his purse.

(6) She knitted a sweater for Tom.

T: We've been friends.

S1: How long have you been friends?

S2: We've been friends since we met at school.

Practice: (1) It is two years.

(2) I have been terribly busy.

(3) She has seldom been out.

(4) Much has change.

(5) It is several.

T: The boys put up their tent in the middle of a field.

S1: Did the boys put up their tent in the middle of a field?

S2: What did the boys do?

S3: Where did the boys put up their tent?

Practice: (1) I got to know her in 1999.

(2) She started her education at a local school.

(3) My grandfather lived a very simple life.

(4) She was married to Tony when she was 21.

(5) He went fishing yesterday.

(6) The conference began at 2 o'clock yesterday.

III Retell the story

Firstly complete the blanks and remember what you said.

Late in the afternoon, the boys _____.
As soon as this was done, they cooked a meal _____.
They were all hungry and the food _____ good. After a
wonderful meal, they _____ by the campfire. But some
time later it began to rain. The boys felt tired so they put out the fire
and _____ their tent. Their sleeping bags were warm and
comfortable, so they all slept _____. In the middle of the night,
two boys _____. The tent was full of water! They all leapt
out of their sleeping bags and hurried outside. It was raining heavily
and they found that a stream had _____ in the field. The stream
_____ the field and then flowed right under their tent!

Secondly retell the story in the third person.

IV Active questions

1. When and where did the boys put up their tent?
2. What did they do and then?
3. Did the food smell delicious?
4. Where did they tell stories and sing songs?
5. What happened some time later?
6. Why did they put out the fire?
7. Were the sleeping bags warm and comfortable?
8. Who woke up in the middle of the night?
9. What was wrong with the tent?
10. What did the boys do?
11. Was it raining heavily?
12. What did the boys find?

Lesson 28

No parking

禁止停车

I **Use the word (s) to make sentence (s)**

Ancient

_____

Ancient — myth

_____ .

Ancient — myth — rare

_____ .

Trouble

_____ .

Trouble — outside

_____ .

Trouble — outside — garden

_____ .

Never

_____ .

Never — dull

_____ .

Never — dull — novel

_____ .

II Practice the key patterns

T: Jasper — rare people — believes in ancient myths
S1: Who is Jasper?
S2: He is one of those rare people who believes in ancient myths.
Practice: (1) he — the only man — robbed him
       (2) the Novel — the best one — I know
       (3) it — the successful book — you ordered
       (4) she — the famous singer — can speak French

T: find a new job
S1: Has she found a new job yet?
S2: Not yet.
S3: Yes, she has.
S1: When did she find it?
S2: Last month.
Practice: (1) move the house
       (2) take my dictionary
       (3) sent some people to help them
       (4) break your cup
       (5) turn out over 2000 cars this month
       (6) make several trips to Paris
       (7) clean his room
       (8) see her this afternoon

T: the friend — knew him
S: The friend who (that) knew him liked him.
Practice: (1) everything — you need
       (2) every time — the telephone rings
       (3) the village — I was born
       (4) the period — I was in London

（5）the postcard — I sent you

（6）Peter — had been driving all day

（7）fruit — pickers — were college students

III Retell the story

Firstly complete the blanks and remember what you said.

Jasper White is one of _____. He has just bought a new _____ in the city, but ever since he moved in, he has had _____ cars and their owners. When he returns home at night, he always finds that _____. Because of this, he has not been _____ to get his own car into his garage even once. Jasper has _____ 'No Parking' signs outside his gate, but these have not _____. Now he has put an ugly stone head over the gate. It is one of the ugliest faces _____. I asked him what it was and he told me that it was Medusa, the Gorgon. Jasper hopes that _____. But none of them has been _____ yet!

Secondly retell the story in the third person.

IV Active questions

1. Who is Jasper White?

2. What has he bought just?

3. What is his trouble with cars and their owners?

4. Has he able to get his own car into his garage once?

5. What action did he take?

6. Has it had effect?

7. What has he done to it and then?

8. Is it the ugliest face?

9. What did you ask him?

10. What did he tell you?

11. What does he hope?

12. Has anybody turned to stone yet?

Lesson 29 Taxi!

出租汽车!

I Use the word (s) to make sentence (s)

Dessert

_____.

Dessert — dangerous

_____.

Dessert — dangerous — trip

_____.

Land

_____.

Land — lonely

_____.

Land — lonely — trip

_____.

Once

_____.

Once — plan

_____.

Once — plan — come true

_____.

II Practice the key patterns

T: surprising — it can land anywhere

S1: What is the most surprising thing?

S2: The most surprising thing is that it can land anywhere.

Practice: (1) surprising — it can fly

(2) exciting — we can win the football match

(3) happiest — I can visit my mother during the Spring Festival

(4) dangerous — they climb the mountain with a heavy bag

(5) important — who is responsible for what has happened

(6) sad — they couldn't agree among themselves

T: I met Kevin last month.

S1: Teacher: When did you meet Kevin?

S2: I met her last month.

S3: Have you met him recently?

S4: No, I haven't met him recently.

Practice: (1) I sent a letter to my mother yesterday.

(2) He gave his son a present last weekend.

(3) I painted the house last week.

(4) The plane took off at nine.

T: We've been friends ever since we met at school.

S1: How long have you been friends?

S2: For 10 years.

S3: We were friends 10 years ago.

Practice: (1) It is two years since I left home.

(2) I have been busy since I've been back.

(3) Much has changed since I was there last time.

(4) It is some time since I have written to her.

(5) We've been living in this city since 1998.

(6) They have been quarrelling ever since they got married.

(7) It has been raining since you came here.

III Retell the story

Firstly complete the blanks and remember what you said.

Captain Ben Fawcett has bought _____ and has begun a new service. The 'taxi' is a small Swiss _____ called a 'Pilatus Porter'. This wonderful plane can _____.

_____ thing about it, however, is that it can land anywhere: on snow, water, or even on a _____ field. Captain Fawcett's first passenger was a doctor _____

_____. Since then, Captain Fawcett has flown passengers to many unusual places. Once he landed _____ of a block of flats and on another occasion, he landed in a _____ car park. Captain Fawcett has just refused a strange _____ from a businessman. The man wanted to fly to Rockall, _____

_____, but Captain Fawcett did not take him because _____

_____.

Secondly retell the story in the third person.

IV Active questions

1. What has Captain Ben Fawcett bought?

2. What is the 'taxi' like?

3. How many passengers can the plane carry?

4. What is the most surprising thing?

5. Where can it land?

6. Who is Captain Fawcett's first passenger?

7. Where did he fly?

8. Has Captain Fawcett refuse a strange request?

9. What is the businessman's request?

10. Why did Captain Fawcett refuse him?

Lesson 30

Football or polo?
足球还是水球?

I Use the word (s) to make sentence (s)

Prefer

_____ .

Prefer — football

_____ .

Prefer — football — polo

_____ .

Kick

_____ .

Kick — ball

_____ .

Kick — ball — bank

_____ .

Sight

_____ .

Sight — realize

_____ .

Sight — realize — happen

_____ .

II Practice the key patterns

T: polite — everyone likes her

S1: She is so polite that everyone likes her.

S2: She is such a polite girl that everyone likes her.

Practice: (1) beautiful — many people crowded around them

(2) noisy — I can't hear what they said

(3) exciting — many people moved to tears

(4) similar — I can't differentiate them

(5) fast — other students can't catch up with him

T: see — passing my house

S1: What did you see yesterday?

S2: I saw him passing my house yesterday?

Practice: (1) hear — striking

(2) watch — rehearing the play

(3) catch — stealing her apples

(4) notice — standing at the door

(5) hear — entering the room

(6) feel — beating fast

T: Ten minutes to walk there.

S1: How long did it take you to walk there?

S2: It took me ten minutes.

S1: Really? It is faster than I do.

Practice: (1) an hour to type the paper

(2) two days to finish the task

(3) one hour to prepare the meeting

(4) thirty minutes to mend the watch

(5) one year to build the bridge

III Retell the story

Firstly complete the blanks and remember what you said.

The Wayle is a small river that _____ . I like sitting by the Wayle on fine afternoons. It was warm last Sunday, so I went and _____ the river bank as usual. Some children were _____ on the bank and there were some people _____ on the river. Suddenly, one of the children kicked a ball very hard and it went towards a passing boat. Some people on the bank _____ the man in the boat, but he did not hear them. The ball _____ him so hard that he nearly fell into the water. I _____ look at the children, but there weren't any _____ : they had all _____ ! The man laughed when he _____ . He called out to the children and _____ _____ back to the bank.

Secondly retell the story in the third person.

IV Active questions

1. What is the Wayle?
2. Where is it?
3. When do you like sitting by the Wayle?
4. What was the weather like last Sunday?
5. What did you do last Sunday?
6. Where were some children playing games?
7. What were some people doing?
8. What happened suddenly?
9. Who called out to the man in the boat?
10. Did he hear them?
11. Why did he nearly fall into the water?

12. Where were they and then?

13. What did the man do when he realized what had happened?

14. What did he do then?

15. What do you think of the children?

Success story
成功者的故事

I Use the word (s) to make sentence (s)

Succeed

_____.

Succeed — company

_____.

Succeed — company — business

_____.

Employ

_____.

Employ — staff

_____.

Employ — staff — enlarge

_____.

Save

_____.

Save — money

_____.

Save — money — experience

_____.

II Practice the key patterns

T: work fourteen hours a day — building his own business

S1: What did he use to do?

S2: He used to work fourteen hours a day.

S1: What is he doing now?

S2: He is the head of a very large business company, he is building his own business now.

Practice: (1) drink beer — working for a famous bank

(2) play PC games — doing his homework

(3) write novels — writing love stories

(4) do morning exercise — sleeping at home

(5) do voluntary work — walking with the dog in the park

T: this morning — doing experiments in the lab

S1: What were you doing this morning? Your mother wanted to see you at home.

S2: I was doing experiments in the lab. I will go home soon.

Practice: (1) at that moment — preparing the exam

(2) at four o'clock — having a bath

(3) when I rang you up — sitting alone on the desk

(4) yesterday afternoon — watering the flowers

(5) at five o'clock yesterday — seeing the doctor

T: kind — help

S1: It was kind of you to help us.

S2: You were kind to help us.

Practice: (1) silly — trust

(2) generous — contribute

(3) unfair — say

(4) annoying — damage

（5）selfish — eat

（6）happy — visit

III Retell the story

Firstly complete the blanks and remember what you said.

Yesterday afternoon Frank Hawkins was telling me about _____ _____ as a young man. Before he _____, Frank was the _____ _____ of a very large business company, but as a boy he _____ _____. It was his job to _____ and at that time he used to work fourteen hours a day. He _____ for years and in 1958 he bought a small workshop of his own. In his twenties Frank used to _____. At that time he had two helpers. In a few years the small workshop had _____ which employed seven hundred and twenty-eight people. Frank smiled when _____ and the long road to success. He was _____ _____ when the door opened and his wife came in. She wanted him to _____!

Secondly retell the story in the third person.

IV Active questions

1. Who was telling you about his experiences as a young man?

2. When did he tell you about it?

3. When was Frank the head of a very large business company?

4. What did he use to do as a boy?

5. How many hours did he use to work?

6. What is his job at that time?

7. When did he buy a small workshop?

8. When did he make spare parts for aeroplanes?

9. How many helpers did he have at that time?

10. Did the small workshop become a large factory in a few years?

11. How many people did he employ?

12. Why did he smile?

13. Who came in?

14. What did she want him to do?

Lesson

32

Shopping made easy
购物变得很方便

I Use the word (s) to make sentence (s)

Once

_____.

Once — temptation

_____.

Once — temptation — parcel

_____.

Buy

_____.

Buy — article

_____.

Buy — article — supermarket

_____.

Detective

_____.

Detective — catch

_____.

Detective — catch — arrest

_____.

Ⅱ Practice the key patterns

T: People are so honest.

S1: We think people are so honest.

S2: No, they are not so honest as they once were.

S3: No, they are not as honest as they once were.

Practice: (1) The situation is so bad.

(2) His opinion is so valuable.

(3) Petrol is so expensive.

(4) He is so handsome.

(5) The food was so good.

(6) Your coffee is so sweet.

T: run — as… as

S1: Did Kevin win the race?

S2: Yes, he ran as quickly as possible.

Practice: (1) finish — as… as

(2) go home — as… as

(3) pick the apple — as… as

(4) talk — as… as

T: There isn't much I can do to help her.

S1: What do you mean?

S2: I mean there is little I can do to help her.

S3: I mean there isn't much I can do to help her.

Practice: (1) There isn't much water in the glass.

(2) There aren't many people here.

(3) You can drink some beer in the bottle.

(4) There is little soup in the bowl.

(5) You can choose many titles to write.

III Retell the story

Firstly complete the blanks and remember what you said.

People are not _____ they once were. The temptation to _____ is greater than ever before — especially in large shops. A detective recently watched _____ who always went into a large store on Monday mornings. One Monday, there were _____ people in the shop than usual when the woman came in, so it _____. The woman first bought a few small articles. After a little time, she _____ one of the _____ _____ dresses in the shop and handed it to an assistant who _____ as quickly as possible. Then the woman simply took the parcel and _____ without paying. When she was arrested, the detective found out _____ ____. The girl 'gave' her mother a free dress _____ a week!

Secondly retell the story in the third person.

IV Active questions

1. Are people as honest as they once were?
2. What is greater than ever before?
3. Whom did the detective watch?
4. When did the woman go into a large store always?
5. Were there many people in the shop on that Monday?
6. Was it easy for the detective to watch her?
7. What did the woman do first?
8. What did she do after a little time?
9. Who did she hand it to?
10. What did the shop assistant do?
11. What did she do then?
12. What is the relationship between the woman and the shop assistant?
13. What did the shop assistant do once a week?

Lesson 33

Out of the darkness

冲出黑暗

I Use the word (s) to make sentence (s)

Struggle

_____.

Struggle — stop

_____.

Struggle — stop — criminal

_____.

Cliff

_____.

Cliff — rock

_____.

Cliff — rock — storm

_____.

Explain

_____.

Explain — dark

_____.

Explain — dark — hole

_____.

Ⅱ Practice the key patterns

T: use your telephone

S1: Would you mind my using your telephone?

S2: OK, go ahead.

S3: Can I use your telephone?

S4: Sorry, there is something wrong with my telephone.

Practice: (1) borrow your pencil

(2) put the box here

(3) help me care the baby

(4) sleep in this house

(5) set the table

(6) keep people out of the garden

T: go for a ride on my bike — off

S1: I am going for a ride on my bike this morning.

S2: Be careful not to fall off!

Practice: (1) go skating — over

(2) work on the cliff — through

(3) go climbing — down

(4) go fishing — in

T: three hours — clean the classroom

S1: I spent three hours in cleaning the classroom.

S2: I spent three hours cleaning the classroom

Practice: (1) three thousand dollars — furniture

(2) two days — travel in that area

(3) half an hour — discuss the problem

(4) one day — tour the lake district

(5) six years — study English

III Retell the story

Firstly complete the blanks and remember what you said.

Nearly a week passed before the girl was able to explain _____

_____. One afternoon she _____ from the

coast in a small boat and was _____. Towards evening,

the boat _____ a rock and the girl _____ the sea. Then

she _____ after spending the whole night in the

water. During that time she _____ eight miles.

Early next morning, she saw a _____ ahead. She knew she was

near the shore because _____. On arriving at

the shore, the girl _____ the cliff towards the light she had

seen. _____. When she woke up a day later, she

found herself in hospital.

Secondly retell the story in the third person.

IV Active questions

1. When was the girl able to explain what had happened to her?

2. Where did the girl set out from one afternoon?

3. What happened to her that evening?

4. When did the boat strike the rock?

5. What did the girl do?

6. How long did she spend in the water?

7. How far did she cover?

8. What did she see early next morning?

9. Why did she know she was near the shore?

10. What did she do on arriving at the shore?

11. Did she remember anything else?

12. When did she wake up?

13. Where was she when she woke up?

Lesson 34

Quick work

破案"神速"

I Use the word (s) to make sentence (s)

Police

_____ .

Police — catch

_____ .

Police — catch — thieve

_____ .

Rather

_____ .

Rather — require

_____ .

Rather — require — trip

_____ .

Expect

_____ .

Expect — surprising

_____ .

Expect — surprising — find

_____ .

II Practice the key patterns

T: travel on business if I am accepted

S1: How often should I travel on business if I am accepted?

S2: Once a month.

S3: It depends. Generally speaking, you should travel on business once a month.

Practice: (1) work overtime

(2) come back

(3) do exercise

(4) have an English class

(5) see a dentist

(6) have a business meeting

T: wash the dishes

S1: I must hurry up. Mother asked me to wash the dishes.

S2: Don't worry. I've washed the dishes for you.

S1: What a surprise! I didn't expect it to have been washed.

Practice: (1) water the garden

(2) deliver the handbag

(3) answer the telephone

(4) air the room

(5) repair the bicycle

(3) make the coffee

T: The maths teacher seems partial towards bright students.

S1: What are they talking about?

S2: It is said that the maths teacher seems partial towards bright students.

Practice: (1) My boss will attend this meeting.

(2) Susan broke the window in the bank.

(3) The drama club will put on a Shakespearean play next Monday.

(4) The company will run as usual.

Ⅲ Retell the story

Firstly complete the blanks and remember what you said.

Dan Robinson has been _____ all week. Last Tuesday he __ _____ from the local police. In the letter he _____ _____. Dan wondered why he was wanted by the police, but he went to the station yesterday and now he is not worried _____. At the station, he was told by a smiling policeman that _____ _____. Five days ago, the policeman told him, the bicycle was _____ up in a small village _____. It is now being _____ his home by train. Dan was most surprised when he _____. He was amused too, because he never _____. It was stolen twenty years ago when Dan was a boy of fifteen!

Secondly retell the story in the third person.

Ⅳ Active questions

1. How long has Dan Robinson been worried?

2. What did he receive last Tuesday?

3. What did the letter say?

4. Why did Dan wonder?

5. When did he go to the station?

6. What was he told at the station?

7. Where was his bicycle picked up?

8. When was it picked up?

9. How is the bicycle being sent?

10. Why was he amused as well?

11. When was the bicycle stolen?

12. How old was he at that time?

35 Stop thief!

捉贼!

I Use the word (s) to make sentence (s)

Regret

_____.

Regret — act

_____.

Regret — act — rudely

_____.

Fright

_____.

Fright — rush

_____.

Fright — rush — straight

_____.

Shortly

_____.

Shortly — battered

_____.

Shortly — battered — run away

_____.

II Practice the key patterns

T: have supper

S1: Have you had supper yet?

S2: Yes, I have.

S1: When did you have it?

S2: Just now.

Practice: (1) the rain stops

(2) see him

(3) make several trips

(4) phone her

(5) wash your car

(6) get a letter from my aunt

T: cook the dinner at home — eat out

S1: He used to cook the dinner at home, didn't he?

S2: Yes, he did. But now he always eats out.

Practice: (1) visit his grandparents twice a week — visit them every week

(2) go to work by subway — walk to work

(3) have a good rest at noon — go swimming

(4) go to bed early — go to bed late

(5) contact with his pen friends on Mondays — contact with them on Sundays

T: suggest — bring the meeting to an end

S1: What is his suggestion?

S2: He suggested that you should bring the meeting to an end.

S3: He suggested bringing the meeting to an end.

Practice: (1) admit — take the money

(2) avoid — over — eat

(3) couldn't help — laugh

(4) detest — look at snakes

(5) advise — take a different approach

(6) mind — move the car

(7) practise — sing the new song

(8) deny — make any statement to that effect

III Retell the story

Firstly complete the blanks and remember what you said.

Roy Trenton used to _____. A short while ago, however, he became a bus driver and he has not _____ it. He is finding his new work _____. When he was driving along Catford Street recently, he saw two thieves rush out of a shop and run towards a waiting car. One of them was carrying a bag full of money. Roy acted quickly and drove the bus straight at the thieves. The one with the money got such a fright that he dropped the bag. As the thieves were trying to get away in their car, Roy drove his bus into the back of it. While the battered car was moving away, Roy stopped his bus and telephoned the police. The thieves' car was badly damaged and easy to recognize. Shortly afterwards, the police stopped the car and both men were arrested.

Secondly retell the story in the third person.

IV Active questions

1. What did Roy Trenton use to do?

2. When did he become a bus driver?

3. Has he regretted this kind of change?

4. Is his job far more exciting?

5. Where was he driving recently?

6. Who rushed out of a shop?

7. Where did he run?

8. What was one of them carrying?

9. What did Roy do?

10. Who got a fright? And what did he do then?

11. Did Roy telephone the police?

12. How to recognize the thieves' car?

13. What happened shortly afterwards?

Lesson

36

Across the Channel
横渡海峡

I Use the word (s) to make sentence (s)

Record

_____ .

Record — break

_____ .

Record — break — swimming

_____ .

Intend

_____ .

Intend — train

_____ .

Intend — train — succeed

_____ .

Gold

_____ .

Gold — solid

_____ .

Gold — solid — liquid

_____ .

Ⅱ Practice the key patterns

T: Debbie's mother — swam the Channel herself

S: Among them will be Debbie's mother, who swam the Channel herself when she was a girl.

Practice: (1) the girl — served in the shop

(2) the boy — spoke in the meeting

(3) anyone — look after him

(4) Peter — everyone suspected

(5) Helen — was sitting beside me

(6) Mrs. Green — lives in the next flat

T: publish this book next week

S1: Is it true that you intend to publish this book?

S2: Yes, it is. I am going to publish it next week.

Practice: (1) rent your house tomorrow

(2) tell her the truth at the next meeting

(3) travel to England next August

(4) fly to Paris tomorrow

(5) cross the border soon

(6) send off the invitation

T: We will announce the results until 6 o'clock.

S1: When will you announce the results?

S2: The results will be announced until 6 o'clock.

S3: We will announce the results until 6 o'clock.

Practice: (1) My mother allowed me to go with you.

(1) His behaviors is troubling me.

(1) We are investigating this car.

(1) They sent the old man to the hospital.

(1) The workers must have built the pagoda in the Ming Dynasty.

III Retell the story

Firstly complete the blanks and remember what you said.

Debbie Hart is going to _____ the English Channel tomorrow. She is going to _____ from the French coast at five o'clock in the morning. Debbie is only eleven years old and she hopes to _____. She is a strong swimmer and many people feel that she is sure to _____. Debbie's father will set out with her in a small boat. Mr. Hart has _____ his daughter for years. Tomorrow he will be _____ _____. Debbie intends to take short rests every _____. She will have something to drink but she will not eat any _____ food. Most of Debbie's school friends will be waiting for her on the _____ ___. Among them will be Debbie's mother, _____.

Secondly retell the story in the third person.

IV Active questions

1. Who's going to swim across the English Channel tomorrow?
2. Where's she going to set out from?
3. When will she set out?
4. How old is Debbie?
5. What does she hope to do?
6. Is she a strong swimmer?
7. Do many people think she'll succeed?
8. Who will set out with her?
9. Will he swim or go in a small boat?
10. How long has he trained Debbie?
11. How will he be watching her tomorrow?
12. Is it a short distance from France to England?
13. How often does Debbie intend to take a rest?

The Olympic Games
奥林匹克运动会

I *Use the word (s) to make sentence (s)*

Hold

_____.

Hold — Olympic

_____.

Hold — Olympic — Beijing

_____.

Immense

_____.

Immense — stadium

_____.

Immense — stadium — hotel

_____.

Design

_____.

Design — capital

_____.

Design — capital — new look

_____.

Ⅱ Practice the key patterns

T: Beijing will hold the Olympic Games this year.

S1: I hear that Beijing will hold the Olympic Games this year.

S2: Yes, the Olympic Games will be held in Beijing this year.

Practice: (1) We will finish the survey next year.

(2) Susan will hand in her essay on Monday.

(3) We will take an English examination next month.

(4) They will furniture the room tomorrow.

T: be on duty

S1: Who will be on duty at six?

S2: I will.

S1: Will you be on duty at six. You said you would go swimming at six.

S2: Oh, sorry, I forgot it.

Practice: (1) be free

(2) know the result

(3) tell me the answer

(4) type this paper for me

(5) come with me

(6) be back

T: my dog — temper — often bite judges

S: My dog, whose temper is very uncertain, often bites judges at dog shows.

Practice: (1) Anne — children — want to get a job

(2) Harry — classmate — help the other students

(3) Kate — car — died in the earthquake

(4) Mr. Black — daughter — was very generous

III Retell the story

Firstly complete the blanks and remember what you said.

The Olympic Games will be held in our country _____ _____. As a great many people will be _____ the country, the government will be _____, an immense stadium, and a new _____ swimming pool. They will also be building new roads and _____. The Games will be held just outside the capital and the whole area will be called 'Olympic City'. _____. By the end of next year, they will have finished work on the _____ ____. The fantastic modern buildings have been _____ by Kurt Gunter. Everybody will be watching anxiously as the new buildings go up. We are all very excited and _____ because they have never been held before in this country.

Secondly retell the story in the third person.

IV Active questions

1. What will be held in our country?
2. When will they be held?
3. How many people will be visiting the country?
4. What will the government be building?
5. Where will the games be held?
6. What is 'Olympic City'?
7. When will the workers have completed the new roads?
8. When will they have finished work on the new stadium?
9. Who has designed the modern buildings?
10. What will everyone be doing as the buildings go up?
11. How do we feel?
12. What are we looking forward to?

13. Why are we all very exciting?

V Translation

1. 因为这是我第一次面对这么多人讲话，所以我感到紧张。
2. 我不能待久了，因为我 20 分钟后有个约会。
3. 修建一座水库。
4. 生火
5. 培养性格
6. 专列
7. 专门医院
8. 最近物价在上涨。
9. 我期待着你尽早回复。
10. 我期待着和你见面。

Everything except the weather
唯独没有考虑到天气

I *Use the word(s) to make sentence(s)* · · · · · · · · · · · · · · · · · ·

Retire

_____.

Retire — settle down

_____.

Retire — settle down — complain

_____.

Storm

_____.

Storm — bear

_____.

Storm — bear — bitterly

_____.

Dream

_____.

Dream — scientist

_____.

Dream — scientist — future

_____.

II Practice the key patterns

T: sell the house — leave the country

S1: Harry sold the house and he left the country.

S2: Harry not only sold the house in the end but also left the country.

Practice: (1) continue the play — make the play successful

(2) sign the contract — invest more money

(3) win the football game — break the record

(4) climb the Great Wall — visit the Palace Museum

T: knock at the door — be in the bathroom

S1: Yesterday morning, I knocked at the door, but nobody answered.

S2: I must have been in the bathroom when you knocked at the door.

Practice: (1) phone you — watch TV

(2) shout to you outside your window — do my homework

(3) knock at the door — be in the backyard

(4) visit you — be on business

(5) email your sister — move to a new place

T: buy a new house this year.

S1: Have you bought a new house yet?

S2: No, not yet. I will buy it this year.

Practice: (1) spend their holiday abroad this summer

(2) go to a pet shop this month

(3) go skating in Switzerland this winter

(4) have a day off work this week

(5) overwork tomorrow

III Retell the story

Firstly complete the blanks and remember what you said.

My old friend, Harrison, had lived in the _____ for many

years _____. He had often dreamed of _____
_____ and had planned to _____ in the country.
_____ and went to live there. Almost
immediately he began to _____ the weather, for even
though it was still summer, it rained continually and it was often ____
____ cold. After so many years of sunshine, Harrison _____
____. He acted as if he had never lived in England before. In the
end, it was _____. He had hardly had time to
_____ when he sold the house and left the country. The
dream _____ so many years ended there. Harrison had
thought of everything except the weather.

Secondly retell the story in the third person.

Ⅳ Active questions

1. Who is Harrison?
2. Where did he live before he returned to England?
3. How long had he lived there?
4. What has he planned to do?
5. What did he do after returning?
6. What did he begin to complain about?
7. What was the weather like in summer?
8. Did Harrison get a shock?
9. Had he never lived in England before?
10. Did Harrison realize his dream?
11. What had he not thought of?

Ⅴ Translation

1. 她拿了杯茶舒舒服服地在椅子上坐了下来。
2. 局势已经平静了下来。

3. 他们不断地吵架。
4. 他们已经连续不停地吵了 1 个多小时。
5. 她去世的消息使我吃了一惊。
6. 你的来信使我很惊奇。
7. 她看我的样子好像我是陌生人一样。
8. 看起来好像要下雨似的。
9. 我的感激之情非言语能表达。
10. 谁认识那位树下站着的老人?

Lesson
39

Am I all right?
我是否痊愈？

I Use the word(s) to make sentence(s)

Operation

_____

Operation — successful

_____

Operation — successful — patient

_____ .

Inquire

_____

Inquire — story

_____

Inquire — story — true

_____

Certain

_____

Certain — exchange

_____ .

Certain — exchange — caller

_____ .

II Practice the key patterns

T: Will John Gilbert's operation be successful tomorrow?

S1: He asked whether John Gilbert's operation will be successful the next day.

S2: He didn't tell me whether John Gilbert's operation will be successful or not.

Practice: (1) Will Jim have a job interview next week? (the next week)

(2) Will Susan go on holiday next weekend?

(3) Will Peter meet her parents at the Beijing airport tomorrow morning?

(4) Will the English teacher give us an exam tomorrow?

(5) Will your parents come here tomorrow afternoon?

(6) Will Mr. Black have an operation next Tuesday?

T: went to the station

S1: What did you say just now?

S2: I said that I went to the station yesterday afternoon.

Practice: (1) traveled to England last summer

(2) filled out this form last night

(3) attended the lecture yesterday

(4) finished this essay last month

(5) waited for your answer yesterday morning

T: Susan — come to class

S1: Has Susan come to class?

S2: Kevin wants to know if Susan has come to class.

Practice: (1) Sam — go to see the dentist

(2) Peter — hand in the English paper

(3) Tim — leave Tianjing

(4) Mary — post the card

（5）Kate — prepare the exam

Ⅲ Retell the story

Firstly complete the blanks and remember what you said.

　　While John Gilbert was in hospital, he asked his doctor to tell him _____, but the doctor _____ so. The following day, the patient asked for a _____. When he was alone, he telephoned the hospital exchange and asked for Doctor Millington. When the doctor _____ the phone, Mr. Gilbert said he was _____, a Mr. John Gilbert. He asked if Mr. Gilbert's operation had been successful and the doctor told him _____. He then asked when Mr. Gilbert would be allowed to go home and the doctor told him that he would have to _____. Then Dr. Millington asked the caller if he was a _____. 'No,' the patient answered, 'I am Mr. John Gilbert.'

Secondly retell the story in the third person.

Ⅳ Active questions

1. Where was John Gilbert?
2. What did he ask his doctor to do?
3. Did the doctor refuse to tell him?
4. What did the patient do the following day?
5. Who did he ask for?
6. Who answered the phone?
7. What did he say on the phone?
8. What did he ask?
9. Did the doctor tell him about the operation?
10. Did he ask if he would be allowed to go home?

11. What about his operation?

12. What was the doctor's reply?

13. What did the doctor ask him?

14. Who was he actually?

V Translation

1. 他希望自己能赢，我也是这么希望。

2. 假如你这么说，那我也只好相信了。

3. 你准备好了么？准备好了，我们就走吧。

4. 我想打听一下航班的情况。

5. 我们会尽快调查此事。

6. 她向我问候我母亲的健康状况。

7. 我已经喝了一杯啤酒了，准备再去要一杯。

8. 关于这个我们另外再找个时间讨论。

9. 我还有几个问题要问。

10. 还有一件事，等你到了那里请把你的地址告诉我。

Lesson
40

Food and talk
进餐与交谈

I Use the word(s) to make sentence(s)

Holiday

_____ .

Holiday — in Hawaii

_____ .

Spend — holiday — in Hawaii

_____ .

Busy

_____ .

Busy — edit

_____ .

Busy — edit — in the office

_____ .

Trouble

_____ .

Trouble — finish

_____ .

Trouble — finish — last week

_____ .

II *Practice the key patterns*

  T: Allen — watch a movie — this Sunday

S1: What will Allen do this Sunday?

S2: Allen will watch a movie this Sunday.

S3: When is Allen going to watch a movie?

S4: This Sunday Allen is going to watch a movie.

S5: Who is to watch a movie this Sunday?

S6: Allen is to watch a movie this Sunday.

Practice: (1) The professor — make a speech — tomorrow

  (2) The monitor — join the sports meeting — next month

  (3) They — go for a trip — the day after tomorrow

  (4) Jane — enter college — next semester

  T: Jennifer's father — lost his watch — last night

S1: When did Jennifer's father lose his watch?

S2: Jennifer's father lost his watch last night.

S3: What happened to Jennifer's father last night?

S4: Jennifer's father lost his watch last night.

Practice: (1) The headmaster — give a lecture — last week

  (2) His aunt — fly to France — yesterday

  (3) My best friend — have an operation — last year

  (4) Our class — have a spring outing — the day before yesterday

  T: asked — would go to that company

S1: If he asked you to, would you go to that company?

S2: I would go to that company if he asked me to.

S3: What would you do if he asked you to?

S4: I would go to that company.

S5: Will you go to that company?

S6: I would go to that company if he asked me to.

Practice: (1) received the invitation — would go to the wedding
　　　　　　　ceremony

　　　　　(2) heard the news — would go to see her

　　　　　(3) had free time — would come with them

　　　　　(4) it was sunny — would go for a picnic

Ⅲ Retell the story

Firstly complete the blanks and remember what you said.

　　Last week at ＿＿＿＿＿＿＿, the hostess asked me to ＿＿＿
＿＿＿＿＿＿＿＿. Mrs Rumbold was a ＿＿＿＿＿＿＿＿＿＿
lady in a tight black dress. She did not even ＿＿＿＿ when I took
my seat beside her. Her eyes were ＿＿＿＿＿＿＿＿＿ and in a
short time, she was busy eating. I ＿＿＿＿＿＿＿＿＿＿.

　　'A new play is coming to "The Globe" soon,' I said. 'Will
you be ＿＿＿＿ it?'

　　'No,' she answered. 'Will you be ＿＿＿＿＿＿＿＿＿
＿＿＿ this year?' I asked.

　　'No,' she answered. 'Will you be staying in England?' I asked.

　　'No,' she answered. In despair, I asked her whether she was

＿＿＿＿＿＿＿＿＿.

　　'Young man,' she answered, 'if you ＿＿＿＿＿＿＿＿＿
＿＿＿, we would both enjoy our dinner!'

Secondly retell the story in the third person.

Ⅳ Active questions

1. Where did this story happen?

2. Why did the writer sit next to Mrs Rumbold?

3. What did Mrs. Rumbold look like?

4. Did Mrs Rumbold look up when the writer sit next to her?

5. What was Mrs Rumbold doing when the writer sit next to her?

6. What did the writer try to do?

7. Will Mrs Rumbold see the new play?

8. What did the writer feel when he heard three "No"?

9. What did Mrs. Rumbold reply when she was asked whether she was enjoying the dinner?

10. What do you think of Mrs. Rumbold's attitude?

Lesson
41

Do you call that a hat?
你把那个叫帽子吗?

I *Use the word (s) to make sentence (s)*

Remind

_____.

Remind — beautiful

_____.

Remind — beautiful — yesterday

_____.

Angry

_____.

Angry — wait

_____.

Angry — wait — for two hours

_____.

Hurry

_____.

Hurry — start

_____.

Hurry — start — soon

_____.

Ⅱ Practice the key patterns

T: you — get up early

S1: You don't need to get up early tomorrow.

S2: You don't need to get up early tomorrow because tomorrow is Sunday.

S3: You needn't have got up early yesterday.

S4: You needn't have got up early yesterday because yesterday is May Day holiday.

Practice: (1) she — phone the head teacher

(2) they — call for the doctor

(3) my sister — buy a new pair of shoes

(4) George — book the ticket

T: finished — homework

S1: Have you finished your homework yet?

S2: Yes, I finished it the day before yesterday.

Practice: (1) posted — letter

(2) decorate — Christmas tree

(3) read — email

(4) publish — fiction

T: you — deliver the package — busy

S1: Will you deliver the package tomorrow?

S2: Sorry, but tomorrow I am busy with my work.

Practice: (1) Caroline — send the report — see the doctor

(2) she — watch the movie — have a date

(3) Tom — repair the bicycle — attend a meeting

(4) he — come to the party — sick

III Retell the story

Firstly complete the blanks and remember what you said.

'Do you call that a hat?' I said to my wife.

'You needn't be so _____ it,' my wife _____

_____ in the mirror. I sat down on one of those modern chairs

with _____ in it and waited. We had been _____

_____ and my wife was still in front of the mirror.

'We mustn't buy things we don't need,' I _____

____. I _____ saying it almost at once. 'You needn't have said

that,' my wife answered. 'I needn't remind you of _____

_____ you bought yesterday.' 'I find it beautiful,' I said. 'A man

can never have too many ties.' 'And a woman can't have _____

_____,' she answered.

Ten minutes later we walked out of the shop together. My wife

was wearing a hat that _____ !

Secondly retell the story in the third person.

IV Active questions

1. Where were 'I' and 'my wife' in when the story happened?
2. Where did 'I' sit on?
3. What did 'I' remark suddenly?
4. What did 'I' regret doing?
5. What did 'my wife' answer to 'my' remark?
6. What did 'I' thought of the tie bought yesterday?
7. When did the couple walk out of the shop?
8. What did the hat look like?

Not very musical

并非很懂音乐

I Use the word (s) to make sentence (s)

Walk

_____.

Walk — market

_____.

Walk — market — square

_____.

Surprise

_____.

Surprise — pick

_____.

Surprise — pick — pocket

_____.

Continue

_____.

Continue — play

_____.

Continue — play — stage

_____.

Ⅱ Practice the key patterns

T: go for a picnic — a fine day

S1: Why not go for a picnic?

S2: Sure. It is a fine day!

S3: We should go for a picnic because it is a fine day.

Practice: (1) join the singing contest — good at singing

(2) see Jack off — our best friend

(3) make an apology — break the window

(4) speak quietly — in the library

T: a heavy smoker — give up smoking

S1: He used to be a heavy smoker.

S2: How is he doing now?

S3: He has given up smoking.

Practice: (1) a party planner — a senior lawyer

(2) live in New York — move to California

(3) be late for class — go to class on time

(4) be very fat — exercise in the gym

T: enjoy the party — the food be awful

S1: Did you enjoy the party last night?

S2: Not really, because the food was awful.

Practice: (1) get the job — fail the interview

(2) go to the concert — work on the project

(3) visit the Great Wall — take care of the baby

(4) receive the letter — be out

Ⅲ Retell the story

Firstly complete the blanks and remember what you said.

As we had _____ one of the markets of

Old Delhi, we stopped at a square to _____. After a time, we noticed _____ with two large baskets _____ _____, so we went to have a look at him. As soon as he saw us, he _____ which was covered with coins and opened one of the baskets. When he began to play a tune, we had our first glimpse of the snake. It _____ and began to _____ of the pipe. We were very much _____ when the snake charmer suddenly began to _____ _____. The snake, however, _____ ____. It obviously could not _____ between Indian music and jazz!

Secondly retell the story in the third person.

Ⅳ Active questions

1. Where did we stop to have a rest?

2. What did we notice at the other side of the square?

3. What did the snake charmer do as soon as he saw us?

4. What was the long pipe covered with?

5. When did we have our first glimpse of the snake?

6. Were we surprised when the snake charmer suddenly began to play jazz?

7. What did the snake continue to do?

8. Do you think that the snake was very musical?

Ⅴ Translate the following sentences into English

1. 昨天他提醒我归还图书馆的书。

2. 他昨天没来上课是因为他得了重感冒。

3. 并不是所有的人都擅长画画的。

4. 让我吃惊的是，他来我们学校前在美国生活了 4 年。

5. 我们原本以为这是一部非常好看的电影。

6. 他没意识到自己已经犯下了一个严重的错误。

7. 要是明天下雨，运动会就取消。

8. 课余时间里我读很多世界名著。

Fully insured

全保险

I *Use the word (s) to make sentence (s)*

Seem

_____.

Seem — happy

_____.

Seem — happy — win

_____.

Paint

_____.

Paint — skillful

_____.

Paint — skillful — contest

_____.

Arrest

_____.

Arrest — steal

_____.

Arrest — steal — shop

_____.

II Practice the key patterns

T: swim — be afraid of water

S1: Can you swim?

S2: I can't, because I am afraid of water.

S3: I'm not able to swim because I am afraid of water.

Practice: (1) speak French — have no time to study

(2) recite the essay — memory is bad

(3) play the piano — too difficult

(4) paint the wall — too busy

T: get up late — miss the bus

S1: what will happen if you get up late?

S2: I will miss the bus if I get up late.

Practice: (1) eat too much food — get sick

(2) watch too much TV — suffer from short sight

(3) not work hard — fail the exam

(4) have a quarrel with the boss — be fired

T: live in this town — for ten years

S1: Do you live in this town?

S2: Yes. I have been living in this town for ten years.

Practice: (1) work in the post office — for a long time

(2) study in the U. S. A. — for more than two years

(3) look after the sick grandma — since six months ago

(4) keep a dog — for about three years

III Retell the story

Firstly complete the blanks and remember what you said.

In _____ , three years after his flight over _____
the American explorer, R. E. Byrd, successfully _____

_____ for the first time. Though, at first, Byrd and his men were able to _____ that lay below, they soon _____. At one point, it seemed certain that their plane would _____. It could only get over the mountains if it rose to _____ feet. Byrd at once ordered his men to _____ _____. The plane was then able to rise and it _____ _____. Byrd now knew that he would be able to reach the South Pole which was _____ away, for there were no more mountains in sight. The aircraft was able to _____ _____ without difficulty.

Secondly retell the story in the third person.

Ⅳ Active questions

1. When did Byrd successfully fly over the South Pole for the first time?

2. When did he fly over the North Pole?

3. At first, what were they able to do?

4. Did they soon run into serious trouble?

5. Was it certain that their plane would crash?

6. What did Byrd order his men to do?

7. Why did he think that he would be able to reach the South Pole?

8. What do you think of Byrd and his men?

Lesson 44

Through the forest
穿过森林

I *Use the word (s) to make sentence (s)*

Mend

_____.

Mend — broken

_____.

Mend — broken — on Monday

_____.

Drop

_____.

Drop — run

_____.

Drop — run — as soon as

_____.

Notice

_____.

Notice — thief

_____.

Notice — thief — fight

_____.

II Practice the key patterns

T: be very tired — continue to run

S1: She was tired, but she continued to run.

S2: She continued to run, though she was very tired.

Practice: (1) be very poor — buy a gift for his wife

(2) get sick — go to work

(3) win Nobel Prize three times — be modest

(4) be thin and short — be good at running

T: water the garden — cook the dinner

S1: I can't water the garden while I cook the dinner.

S2: OK. I will water the garden while you cook the dinner.

Practice: (1) go sightseeing — work on the program

(2) clean the kitchen — take care of the baby

(3) edit the manuscript — plan the schedule

(4) write the report — comment on the novel

T: miss the bus — take a cab

S1: What would you do if you miss the bus?

S2: I would take a cab if I miss the bus.

Practice: (1) be on a holiday — see my grandparents

(2) lose your way — ask the policeman

(3) fail the exam — work harder

(4) it rains — try to borrow an umbrella

III Retell the story

Firstly complete the blanks and remember what you said.

Mrs. Anne Sterling did not think of _____

_____ when she ran through a forest after two men. They had rushed up to her while she was _____ with her

children and tried to steal her handbag. In the struggle, _____
_____ and, with the bag in their possession, both men started
running through the trees. Mrs. Sterling got _____
____ them. She was soon _____, but she
continued to run. When she _____, she saw that
they had sat down and were _____, so she ran
straight at them. The men _____ that they
dropped the bag and ran away. 'The strap _____
____,' said Mrs. Sterling later, 'but they did not steal anything.'
Secondly retell the story in the third person.

Ⅳ Active questions

1. What happened when Mrs. Sterling was having a picnic?
2. What did the two men try to steal?
3. Where were Mrs. Sterling and her children having dinner?
4. What happened to the strap in the struggle?
5. Did Mrs. Sterling continue to run though she was out of breath?
6. What did she saw when she caught up with the two men?
7. What did Mrs. Sterling said later?
8. What do you think of Mrs. Sterling?

Lesson 45

A clear conscience

问心无愧

I Use the word(s) to make sentence(s)

Wonder

_____.

Wonder — incident

_____.

Wonder — incident — happen

_____.

Return

_____.

Return — wallet

_____.

Return — wallet — thank

_____.

Appreciate

_____.

Appreciate — painting

_____.

Appreciate — painting — gallery

_____.

II Practice the key patterns

T: hand in — the report

S1: What are you going to do this afternoon?

S2: I am going to hand in the report.

S3: Has the report been handed in?

S4: It had been handed in by Lisa yesterday.

Practice: (1) wash — the car

(2) weed — the garden

(3) wash — the dishes

(4) do — the housework

T: go to the library — read

S1: What will you do this Saturday?

S2: I will go to the library this Saturday.

S3: What have you been doing in the library?

S4: I have been reading in the library.

Practice: (1) go to the theater — watch a play

(2) go to the lab — do experiments

(3) go to the laundry — wash the clothes

(4) go to the riverside — fish

T: airport — meet a visiting scholar

S1: Where is Sandy now?

S2: He has gone to the airport to meet a visiting scholar.

Practice: (1) party — have fun

(2) mountains — plant trees

(3) playground — do exercises

(4) restaurant — have dinner

III Retell the story

Firstly complete the blanks and remember what you said.

The whole village soon learnt that _____

had been lost. Sam Benton, the local _____, had lost his wallet while _____ to the post office. Sam was sure that the wallet must _____, but it was not ____ ____ to him. Three months passed, and then one morning, Sam found his wallet outside his front door. It had been _____ _____ and it _____ half the money he had lost, together with a note which said: 'A thief, yes, but only 50 percent a thief!' Two months later, some more money was _____ _____: 'Only 25 percent a thief now!' _____, all Sam's money was _____. The last note said: 'I am 100 percent _____ now!'

Secondly retell the story in the third person.

Ⅳ Active questions

1. How much money had been lost?
2. What was Sam's job?
3. What was Sam sure?
4. How much time had passed before Sam found his wallet?
5. What was the wallet wrapped in?
6. What did the first note say?
7. When did some more money come back with the second note?
8. What did the last note said?

Ⅴ Fill the blanks with the correct form of the verbs given

of, to, up, at, on, off, about, in, for

1. This picture reminds me _____ the old man I met this morning.
2. We are really looking forward _____ your coming to our house.
3. Don't laugh _____ the classmates who are not good at

drawing.

4. On my way home, I picked _____ a watch.

5. Please turn _____ the light. It is dark.

6. Don't worry _____ him! He is safe right now!

7. Can you account _____ the incident last night?

8. Thanks to the firefighters, the big fire was finally put _____ _____.

9. We were very surprised _____ the fact that they were twins.

10. After three months' training, I finally succeed _____ wining the first prize in the singing contest.

Lesson 46

Expensive and uncomfortable 既昂贵又受罪

I Use the word (s) to make sentence (s)

Complain

_____.

Complain — expensive

_____.

Complain — expensive — afford

_____.

Dream

_____.

Dream — fly

_____.

Dream — fly — bird

_____.

Intend

_____.

Intend — trip

_____.

Intend — trip — Malaysia

_____.

II Practice the key patterns

T: the survey — conduct

S1: Do you know when the survey is going to be conducted?

S2: As far as I know, it is being conducted now.

Practice: (1) the issue — discuss

(2) the library — build

(3) the watch — repair

(4) the parcel — check

T: the ground is wet — rain

S1: Look, the ground is wet!

S2: It must have rained last night.

Practice: (1) very happy — win the first prize

(2) get a high score — work hard

(3) fall asleep — be too tired

(4) be late for class — go to bed too late

T: read a book — rush in

S1: What were you doing yesterday when Tom rushed in?

S2: I was reading a book when Tom rushed in.

Practice: (1) listen to music — turn off the light

(2) play chess with Jennifer — rain

(3) check the information — come in

(4) do the homework — the door rings

III Retell the story

Firstly complete the blanks and remember what you said.

When a plane from London arrived at _____,

workers began to _____ a number of wooden boxes which _____

_____. No one could _____ that one of

the boxes was extremely heavy. It suddenly _____ one of the workers to open up the box. He _____ what he found. A man was lying in the box _____. He was so surprised at _____ that he did not even try to run away. After he was arrested, the man _____ before the plane left London. He had had _____ trip, for he had been _____ the wooden box for over eighteen hours. The man was ordered to pay 3500 for the cost of the trip. The normal price of a ticket is 2000!

Secondly retell the story in the third person.

Ⅳ Active questions

1. Where did the plane from London arrive at?
2. What did the wooden boxes contain?
3. What suddenly occurred to one of the workers?
4. What did this worker find?
5. What did the man in the box admit?
6. How about the man's trip?
7. How long had the man been confined to the box?
8. How much money was the man ordered to pay?

A thirsty ghost
嗜酒的鬼魂

Occur

_____.

Occur — check

_____.

Occur — check — right

_____.

Discover

_____.

Discover — buy

_____.

Discover — buy — gift

_____.

Pretend

_____.

Pretend — sick

_____.

Pretend — sick — lazy

_____.

II Practice the key patterns

T: happy — won the first prize

S1: Why Sarah was so happy yesterday?

S2: Because she won the first prize in the composition test yesterday.

Practice: (1) worried — his father had an accident

(2) sad — lost her pen

(3) upset — his secret was discovered

(4) diappointed — got a low score in the exam

T: mend the watch

S1: ·Have you mended the watch?

S2: Not yet. But I will mend it right now.

Practice: (1) lay the table

(2) wash the clothes

(3) read the newspaper

(4) prepare the super

T: do the homework — at eight tomorrow evening

S1: What will you be doing at eight tomorrow evening?

S2: I will be doing my homework.

Practice: (1) visit my old friend — at ten tomorrow morning

(2) have a bathing — at nine tomorrow night

(3) design the ads — at eleven next Monday

III Retell the story

Firstly complete the blanks and remember what you said.

A public house which was recently bought by Mr. Ian Thompson
is _____ . Mr. Thompson is going to sell it because ____
____ . He told me that he could not go to sleep one night because he
heard _____ coming from the bar. The next morning, he

found _____ by chairs and the furniture had been moved. Though Mr. Thompson _____ before he went to bed, they were on in the morning. He also said that he had found five _____ which the ghost must have _____. When I suggested that some villagers must have _____, Mr. Thompson _____. The villagers have told him that they will not accept the pub even if he _____.

Secondly retell the story in the third person.

IV Active questions

1. Why is Mr. Thompson going to sell the pub?
2. What did he hear one night?
3. What did he find the next morning?
4. Were the lights on in the morning?
5. What evidence is there that the ghost must have drunk?
6. What did I suggest to Mr. Thompson?
7. What did he react to my suggestion?
8. Would the villagers accept the pub even if he gives it away?

Lesson 48 Did you want to tell me something?

你想对我说什么吗？

I Use the word (s) to make sentence (s)

Hobby

_____.

Hobby — watch

_____.

Hobby — watch — theatre

_____.

Accept

_____.

Accept — invitation

_____.

Accept — invitation — trip

_____.

Nod

_____.

Nod — answer

_____.

Nod — answer — puzzle

_____.

II Practice the key patterns

T: ask — get back the ticket

S1: What did he ask you to do?

S2: He asked me to get back the ticket.

Practice: (1) advise — go to see the doctor

(2) tell — post the letter

(3) recommend — hand in the report on time

(4) counsel — exchange ideas with others

T: go now — go later

S1: Shall we go now or later?

S2: I'd prefer to go later.

Practice: (1) pick the yellow one — green one

(2) go fishing — go skiing

(3) go by train — go by air

(4) work alone — work with other people

T: go to the art museum

S1: Would you like to go to the art museum?

S2: Not really. To tell the truth, I hate going to the museum.

Practice: (1) buy the cartoon book

(2) watch Shakespeare's play

(3) read the detective fiction

(4) look after the baby

III Retell the story

Firstly complete the blanks and remember what you said.

Dentists always ask questions when it is _____

_____. My dentist had just _____ one of my teeth and had told me to _____. I tried to say something, but my mouth was _____. He knew I collected _____ and asked me whether _____. He then asked me how my brother was and whether I liked my new job in London. In answer to these questions I either _____ or _____. Meanwhile, my tongue was busy _____ where the tooth had been. I suddenly _____, but could not say anything. When the dentist at last _____ the cotton wool from my mouth, I was able to tell him that he had _____

_____.

Secondly retell the story in the third person.

Ⅳ Active questions

1. When do dentists always ask questions?

2. What did my dentist tell me to do after pulling out one of my teeth?

3. What was my mouth full of?

4. What did I collect?

5. What did I do in answer to the questions?

6. What was my tongue busy doing?

7. Finally what was I able to tell the dentist?

8. What do you think of the dentist?

Ⅴ Translate the following sentences into English

1. 难道你不认为他的态度太粗鲁了吗？

2. 虽然下着雨，他们还是冒雨前进。

3. 你知道地震是怎么发生的吗？

4. 请问可以告诉我去体育馆怎么走吗？

5. 去年他肯定去过澳大利亚。

6. 他很担心，怕自己考试过不了。

7. 她非常生气以至于都发脾气了。

8. 如果你迷路该怎么办呢？

9. 这位作家很受年轻人的喜欢。

10. 很显然，他欺骗了他的父母。

The end of a dream
美梦告终

Glimpse

_____.

Glimpse — cat

_____.

Glimpse — cat — noise

_____.

Shake

_____.

Shake — head

_____.

Shake — head — disagree

_____.

Reason

_____.

Reason — fail

_____.

Reason — fail — sick

_____.

II Practice the key patterns

T: happy — jump

S1: Rose looks so happy.

S2: Yes. She is so happy that she jumps.

Practice: (1) terrified — burst into tears

(2) angry — tear the paper into pieces

(3) sad — cannot stop crying

(4) worried — cannot sleep well

T: hand in — the report

S1: You should have handed in your report.

S2: Sorry, I forgot. I will hand it in as soon as possible.

Practice: (1) finish — the experiment

(2) discuss — the problem

(3) write — the letter

(4) return — the book

T: sick — go to school

S1: Why doesn't Jim go to school?

S2: He is too sick to go to school.

Practice: (1) late — catch the bus

(2) sad — say a word

(3) lazy — deliver the parcel

III Retell the story

Firstly complete the blanks and remember what you said.

Tired of _____, a young man in Teheran saved up for years to buy a real bed. For the first time in his life, he became _____ which had springs and a mattress. Because _____, he carried the bed on to the roof of his house. He slept very well for the first two nights, but on the third night, _____. A gust of wind _____ _____ the roof and sent it crashing into the courtyard below. The young man did not wake up until the bed had _____ _____. Although the bed was _____, the man was _____. When he woke up, he was still _____ _____. Glancing at the bits of wood and metal that lay around him, the man sadly _____ and carried it into his house. After he had put it on the floor, he _____ _____ again.

Secondly retell the story in the third person.

Ⅳ Active questions

1. Why the man bought a real bed?
2. What did the bed have?
3. Why did he carry the bed to the roof of his house?
4. Did he sleep well for the first two nights?
5. What happened on the third night?
6. When did the man wake up?
7. Was he hurt?
8. What did the man do after he woke up?
9. What did he do before he went to sleep again?
10. What do you think of the young man?

Lesson 50

Taken for a ride
乘车兜风

I *Use the word (s) to make sentence (s)*

Tired

_____ .

Tired — same

_____ .

Tired — same — decide

_____ .

Accept

_____ .

Accept — invitation

_____ .

Accept — invitation — glad

_____ .

Comment

_____ .

Comment — clothes

_____ .

Comment — clothes — ugly

_____ .

II Practice the key patterns

T: clean the window

S1: What is Emily doing?

S2: She is cleaning the window.

S3: Oh, she should have cleaned it yesterday.

Practice: （1）water the plants

（2）choose the gift for her Mom

（3）buy some milk

（4）feed the pet

T: write the report

S1: Will you come to my house tomorrow?

S2: Sorry, but I have to write the project.

S3: Oh, I thought you have written it.

Practice: （1）send Christmas cards

（2）repair the fridge

（3）climb that mountain

（4）write the thesis

（5）see a dentist

T: finish the assignment — two hours

S1: Did you finish the assignment yesterday?

S2: Yes. I finished it in two hours.

Practice: （1）see a football match — three hours

（2）have a talk with Sam — half an hour

（3）draw a picture — one hour

III Retell the story

Firstly complete the blanks and remember what you said.

I love _____, but I don't like losing my way.

I _____ recently, but my trip took me _____

_____. 'I'm going to Woodford Green,' I said to the

conductor as I got on the bus, 'but I don't know where it is.' 'I'll

tell you where to get off,' answered the conductor. I sat _____

_____ the bus to _____. After some

time, the bus stopped. Looking round, I _____

that I was _____ left on the bus. 'You'll have to

get off here,' the conductor said. 'This is _____

____.' 'Is this Woodford Green?' I asked. 'Oh dear,' said the

conductor _____. 'I forgot to put you off.' 'It doesn't matter,'

I said. 'I'll get off here.' 'We are going back now,' said the

conductor. 'Well, in that case, I _____,' I

answered.

Secondly retell the story in the third person.

Ⅳ *Active questions*

. . . .

1. What do I love doing?

2. What did I say to the conductor as I got on the bus?

3. Why did I sit in the front of the bus?

4. What did I realize after the bus stopped?

5. What did the conductor say suddenly?

6. Does the bus go back now?

7. What did I say at last?

8. Did I prefer to stay on the bus or not?

Reward for virtue
对美德的奖赏

I Use the word (s) to make sentence (s)

Forbid

_____

Forbid — enter

_____

Forbid — enter — after

_____

Own

_____

Own — precious

_____

Own — precious — lend

_____

Nod

_____

Nod — teacher

_____

Nod — teacher — praise

_____

Ⅱ Practice the key patterns

T: write a letter

S1: Did you write a letter to Tim?

S2: Yes. I wrote a letter to Tim two weeks ago.

Practice: (1) phone your cousin

(2) go shopping with your aunt

(3) bake a birthday cake

(4) go to a park

T: tired — work the whole day

S1: Why does she look so tired?

S2: Because she has been working the whole day.

Practice: (1) impatient — wait for three hours

(2) hesitant — consider the problem for two hours

(3) worried — sick for two month

T: wait for them in the airport — buy a magazine

S1: What happened while she was waiting for them in the airport?

S2: She bought a magazine to read while she was waiting for them in the airport.

Practice: (1) walk on the way home — lose his wallet

(2) listen to the radio — knock the door

(3) paint the wall — start to rain

Ⅲ Retell the story

Firstly complete the blanks and remember what you said.

My friend, Hugh, has always been fat, but things got so bad recently that he decided to _____ . He began his diet a week ago. First of all, he _____ which were _____ . The list included most of the things Hugh loves: butter,

potatoes, rice, beer, milk, chocolate, and sweets. Yesterday I _____
_____. I rang the bell and was not surprised to see that Hugh was
still as fat as ever. He led me into his room and _____
under his desk. It was obvious that he was very _____.
When I asked him what hc was doing, he _____ and
then put the parcel on the desk. He explained that his diet was so
strict that he had to _____. Then he showed
me _____. It contained five large bars of
chocolate and three bags of sweets!

Secondly retell the story in the third person.

IV Active questions

1. Recently what did Hugh decide to do?

2. When did he begin his diet?

3. What did he do first of all?

4. What did the list include?

5. What did I do yesterday?

6. What did Hugh hurriedly hide under his desk?

7. What did he explain to me about the parcel?

8. What were the contents of the parcel?

V Fill the blanks with the correct form of the verbs given

1. In order _____ English well, he reads English poets every
   morning. (learn)

2. While _____ in a foreign country, remember to take the
   passport with you all the time. (travel)

3. Money is _____ for buying and selling goods. (use)

4. On Sunday, Bob usually goes _____ with his father.
   (swim)

5. She _____ the whole morning. She is very tired. (work)

6. Last month, they were busy _____ for the wedding ceremony. (prepare)

7. A new product has _____ by this company. (invent)

8. He will be able _____ this poem after three days. (recite)

9. She is very _____ in that book. (interest)

10. They were surprised at _____ that the key was lot. (discover)

I Use the word (s) to make sentence (s)

Decide

_____.

Decide — move

_____.

Decide — move — beautiful

_____

Upset

_____

Upset — sick

_____

Upset — sick — hospital

_____.

Discover

_____.

Discover — steal

_____.

Discover — steal — neighbor

_____.

II Practice the key patterns

· ·

T: sick — be in hospital

S1: You look sick. What is the matter?

S2: I've been in hospital since Tuesday.

Practice: (1) tired — prepare for the debate

(2) upset — go over the lesson for the coming week

(3) worried — worry about dad's heart disease all the time

T: Ashley — visit a museum

S1: Do you know what Ashley did yesterday?

S2: I heard that she visited a museum.

Practice: (1) Mary   have a piano lesson

(2) Elizabeth — read the latest released book

(3) Pauper — see sunrise on the beach

(4) Jack — buy a new pair of sports shoes

T: read the novel

S1: Have they read the whole novel?

S2: Yes, they have. They have read the novel from the beginning to the end.

Practice: (1) finish the whole project

(2) find the lost watch

(3) clean the floor

(4) iron the clothes

III Retell the story

· ·

Firstly complete the blanks and remember what you said.

We have just moved into a new house and I have _____

_____. I have been trying to _____. This has not been easy because I own over a thousand books. _____, the room is rather small, so I have _____. At the moment, they cover every inch of floor space and I actually have to walk on them to _____. A short while ago, my sister helped me to carry one of my old bookcases up the stairs. She went into my room and _____ when she saw all those books on the floor. 'This is the _____ I have ever seen,' she said. She _____ for some time then added, 'You don't need bookcases at all. You can sit here in your spare time and _____ _____!'

Secondly retell the story in the third person.

Ⅳ Active questions

1. What have I been trying to do?
2. How many books do I have?
3. Is the new room big or small?
4. Where do I decide to put the books?
5. Who came to help me carry the bookcase?
6. Was she surprised when she got into my room?
7. What did she say?
8. Why did she say that I didn't need bookcases?

Lesson 53

53 Hot snake

触电的蛇

I *Use the word (s) to make sentence (s)* . . . .

Solve

_____.

Solve — mystery

_____.

Solve — mystery — reason

_____.

Single

_____.

Single — friend

_____.

Single — friend — perish

_____.

Manage

_____.

Manage — save

_____.

Manage — save — fire

_____.

II Practice the key patterns

T: go abroad

S1: Do you know where Joe is now?

S2: He went abroad last year and hasn't come back.

Practice: (1) go to the library

(2) go to the headmaster's room

(3) go hunting

(4) go to the concert

T: hand in the report

S1: Have you handed in the report already?

S2: Not yet. I'll hand it in tomorrow morning.

Practice: (1) return the books — next Monday

(2) write to your pen pal — this Friday

(3) get dressed — soon

(4) water the flowers — in a moment

T: get up early

S1: Are you used to getting up early?

S2: No, I am not. But I think soon I will get used to it.

Practice: (1) stay up late

(2) ride to work

(3) walk alone to the apartment at night

(4) go to the park every evening

III Retell the story

Firstly complete the blanks and remember what you said.

At last firemen have _____ in California. Since then, they have been trying to _____ . Forest fires are often caused by broken glass or by cigarette ends which people ____

_____. Yesterday the firemen examined the ground carefully, but were not able to find any broken glass. They were also quite sure that a cigarette end did not start the fire. This morning, however, a fireman _____. He noticed _____ which was wound round the electric wires of a 16000-volt power line. In this way, he was able to _____. The explanation was simple but very unusual. A bird had _____ from the ground and then dropped it on to the wires. The snake then _____. When it did so, it _____ to the ground and these immediately started a fire.

Secondly retell the story in the third person.

Ⅳ Active questions

1. What have the firemen been trying to find?
2. What are often the causes of forest fires?
3. What are the firemen quite sure?
4. Who accidentally discovered the cause?
5. What was wound round the electric wires of a 16000-volt power line?
6. Was the explanation simple or not?
7. Where did the bird drop the snake?
8. How did the snake send sparks down to the ground?

Lesson 54 Sticky fingers

粘糊的手指

I Use the word(s) to make sentence(s)

Recognize

_____ .

Recognize — own

_____ .

Recognize — own — shirt

_____ .

Persuade

_____ .

Persuade — join

_____ .

Persuade — join — watch

_____ .

Lie

_____ .

Lie — contest

_____ .

Lie — contest — win

_____ .

II Practice the key patterns

T: call the head of the office

S1: Will you call the head of the office today?

S2: I have given him a call yesterday.

Practice: (1) have dinner with the manager

(2) see a dentist

(3) decorate your house

(4) publish your poem

T: Susana — write the essay

S1: What's Susana doing now?

S2: She's writing. She has been writing the essay nonstop since last night.

Practice: (1) Julia — read the fiction

(2) George — discuss something with his best friend

(3) Peter — watch TV

(4) Stephen — cut the grass

T: rent a house

S1: Are you going to rent a house this month?

S2: I don't think so. I rent a house last week.

Practice: (1) bake the pies

(2) attend the seminar

(3) go to Wangfujing Main Street

(4) make a holiday plan

III Retell the story

Firstly complete the blanks and remember what you said.

After breakfast, I sent the children to school and then I _____

_____. It was still early when I returned home. The children

were at school, my husband was at work and the house was quiet. So I decided to _____. In a short time I was _____ _____ and my hands were soon _____.
At exactly that moment, the telephone rang. Nothing could have been _____. I picked up the receiver between _____ _____ and was dismayed when I recognized the voice of Helen Bates. It took me ten minutes to _____. At last I hung up the receiver. What a mess! There was pastry on my fingers, on the telephone, and on the doorknobs. I _____ _____ the doorbell rang _____. This time it was the postman and he wanted me to _____!
Secondly retell the story in the third person.

Ⅳ Active questions

1. What did I do after breakfast?

2. What did I decide to do at the quiet home?

3. In a short time what was I busy doing?

4. What were my hands covered with?

5. How did I pick up the receiver?

6. What did I persuade Helen Bates to do?

7. On which there was pastry?

8. Why did the doorbell ring?

Ⅴ Translate the following sentences into English

1. 他已经习惯了使用筷子。

2. 自去年以来，她一直在研究中国文化。

3. 我忘记把这事告诉她了。

4. 机器人在现实生活中被应用得越来越广。

5. 广场上到处都是人。

6. 这个小城镇得到了快速的发展。

7. 这对夫妻在国外已经呆了 10 多年了。

8. 他目睹了一起交通事故。

9. 我们充分认识到了形势的严峻。

10. 小时候我们常常玩游戏。

55 Not a gold mine
并非金矿

I Use the word(s) to make sentence(s)

Invent

_____.

Invent — new

_____.

Invent — new — find

_____.

Dismayed

_____.

Dismayed — come

_____.

Dismayed — come — on time

_____.

Examine

_____.

Examine — machine

_____.

Examine — machine — quality

_____.

II Practice the key patterns

T: go to pub — be free

S1: Would you like to go to pub tonight?

S2: I'd like to if I am free.

Practice: (1) attend the rehearsal — get up early enough

(2) go jogging in the park — it stops raining

(3) watch an interesting play — you invite me to

(4) play football with us — don't have to work

T: be away from home

S1: How long have you been away from home?

S2: I have been away from home for nearly two years.

Practice: (1) teach English in college

(2) stay in the hospital

(3) exercise in the gym

(4) work in the research center

T: go shopping — hot

S1: Would you like to go shopping with me today?

S2: Sorry. But I think it is too hot to go out.

Practice: (1) help to lift the box — heavy

(2) buy the apartment near the sea — expensive

(3) mend the radio — badly damaged

III Retell the story

Firstly complete the blanks and remember what you said.

Dreams of finding lost treasure almost _____ recently. A new machine called 'The Revealer' has been invented and it has been used to _____ which has been buried in the ground. The machine was used in a cave near the seashore where — it is said —

pirates used to _____. The pirates would often bury gold in the cave and then _____. _____, a search party went into the cave hoping to _____. The leader of the party was examining the soil near the entrance to the cave when the machine showed that there was gold under the ground. Very excited, the party _____. They finally found a small gold coin which was _____. The party then searched the whole cave thoroughly but did not find anything except _____. In spite of this, many people are _____ _____ that 'The Revealer' may reveal something of value fairly soon.

Secondly retell the story in the third person.

Ⅳ Active questions

1. What is the name of the new machine that is used to detect gold?
2. Where did pirates use to hide gold?
3. What would the pirates often do with gold?
4. What did the machine show?
5. How did the party feel?
6. How deep did they dig the hole?
7. What did they find at last?
8. What do many people think of 'The Revealer'?

I Use the word (s) to make sentence (s)

Persuade

_____.

Persuade — accept

_____.

Persuade — accept — invitation

_____.

Allow

_____.

Allow — continue

_____.

Allow — continue — work

_____.

Employ

_____.

Employ — typist

_____.

Employ — typist — workshop

_____.

Ⅱ Practice the key patterns

T: conduct the investigation

S1: Have you finished conducting the investigation?

S2: not yet. I have much trouble in designing the questionnaire.

Practice: (1) do the experiment

(2) write the final report

(3) collect the data

(4) paint the house

T: the gate of the cinema

S1: Where shall we meet today?

S2: I'll wait for you at the gate of the cinema.

Practice: (1) the entrance of the theatre

(2) the square of the park

(3) the hall of the hotel

(4) the exit of the station

T: blame for making many mistakes in the report

S1: Monica was blamed for making many mistakes in the report.

S2: That's not surprising. She is being careless all the time.

Practice: (1) criticize for handing in the thesis too late

(2) scold for making the room messy

(3) sentence to death for killing two people

Ⅲ Retell the story

Firstly complete the blanks and remember what you said.

Once a year, a race is held for _____ . A lot of cars entered for this race last year and there was _____ just before it began. One of the most handsome cars was a Rolls-royce Silver Ghost. The most unusual car was a Benz which _____

_____. Built in 1885, it was the oldest car _____ . After a great many loud explosions, the race began. Many of the cars ____ _____ and some drivers spent more time under their cars than in them! A few cars, however, completed the race. The winning car reached a speed of _____ — much faster than any of its rivals. It sped downhill at the end of the race and its driver had _____ . The race gave everyone __ _____ . It was very _____ _____ but no less exciting.

Secondly retell the story in the third person.

Ⅳ **Active questions**

　　1. How often is a race held for old cars?

　　2. How many cars entered for this race last year?

　　3. What's the name of the most handsome car?

　　4. Which is the most unusual car?

　　5. How many wheels did this car have?

　　6. When was this car built?

　　7. Did many of the cars break down on the course?

　　8. What was the speed of the winning car?

　　9. When did the driver of this car have a lot of trouble?

　　10. Was this race the same as the modern car races?

Lesson 57

Can I help you, madam?
您要买什么，夫人？

I Use the word (s) to make sentence (s)

Punish

_____.

Punish — mistake

_____.

Punish — mistake — project

_____.

Serve

_____.

Serve — customer

_____.

Serve — customer — praise

_____.

Strict

_____.

Strict — task

_____.

Strict — task — salary

_____.

II Practice the key patterns

T: keep a dog — three years

S1: Have you ever kept a dog?

S2: Yes. I kept a dog for three years.

Practice: (1) live beside the sea — nearly six years

(2) study abroad — two years

(3) run a shop — a long time

(4) live with your grandparents — when I was a little kid

T: join our party — work on my project

S1: Are you free tomorrow night? Would you like to join our party?

S2: Sorry. Tomorrow night I'll be working on my project.

Practice: (1) watch a movie — clean the house

(2) attend the meeting — mow the lawn

(3) go for a picnic — prepare for the exam

T: climb the Great Wall — three hours

S1: Did you climb the Great Wall yesterday?

S2: Yes. I spent three hours climbing it.

Practice: (1) work out the plan — two hours

(2) finish the homework — two hours and a half

(3) have a talk with Ross — on hour

(4) ride to work — fifty minutes

III Retell the story

Firstly complete the blanks and remember what you said.

A woman in jeans stood at the window of _____.
Though she _____, she finally went in and asked
to see a dress that was in the window. The assistant who served her
did not like the way she was dressed. _____, he

told her that the dress was sold. The woman walked out of the shop angrily and decided to _____. She returned to the shop the following morning dressed in _____, with a handbag in one hand and _____ in the other. After ____ _____ she asked for the same dress. Not realizing who she was, the assistant was _____. With great difficulty, he _____. As soon as she saw it, the woman said she did not like it. She _____ _____ in the window before finally buying the dress she had first asked for.

Secondly retell the story in the third person.

IV Active questions

1. Where did the woman stand?
2. What did the woman ask for?
3. Did the assistant like the way the women was dressed?
4. How did the assistant glance at her?
5. What did the woman decide to do?
6. What did the woman dress in the next day?
7. Did the assistant recognize her?
8. What did the woman buy finally?

V Fill the blanks with appropriate propositions

1. We didn't go for a picnic because _____ the bad weather.
2. Bob never listens _____ his parents at home.
3. Everyone in the classroom agrees _____ this idea.
4. The baby cried the moment he caught the sight _____ the tiger.
5. She tried very hard to catch up _____ her classmates when

she returned to school.

6. Jack had a fight _____ the new desk — mate.

7. In spite _____ the heavy rain, they started the journey.

8. The customers are not allowed _____ enter this room.

9. He is astonished _____ the news that she intends to go abroad next month.

10. I dreamed _____ becoming a scientist when I was in my childhood.

I Use the word (s) to make sentence (s)

Spend

_____.

Spend — holiday

_____.

Spend — holiday — in Hawaii

_____.

Waste

_____.

Waste — energy

_____.

Waste — energy — meaningless

_____.

Understand

_____.

Understand — difficult

_____.

Understand — difficult — theory

_____.

II Practice the key patterns

T: Lucy — her father died of heart disease

S1: Do you know what had happened to Lucy?

S2: It is said that her father died of heart disease last night.

Practice: (1) Tim — he won the first prize in the contest

(2) Smith — broke his leg while running

(3) Angie — had an accident on the way home

(4) Shelly — gave birth to a girl

T: say — a conference next Wednesday

S1: Excuse me! What did she say just now?

S2: She said that there would be a conference next Wednesday.

Practice: (1) complain — so much work to do every day

(2) say — a spring outing tomorrow

(3) tell you — a storm this evening

T: work — three years

S1: Where do you work now?

S2: In a publishing house. I have been working there for three years.

Practice: (1) study — four years

(2) live — roughly two years

(3) stay — about two months

(4) keep — five months

III Retell the story

Firstly complete the blanks and remember what you said.

The tiny village of Frinley is said to possess a ' _____ '.
Because the tree was mentioned in a newspaper, the number of
visitors to Frinley has now increased. The tree was planted _____
_____ , but it is only in recent years that it has _____
_____ . It is said that if anyone _____

_____, he will have bad luck; if he _____,
he will die. Many villagers believe that the tree has already _____
_____. The vicar has been asked to have the tree cut
down, but so far he has refused. He has pointed out that the tree is
_____, as tourists have been coming from all
parts of the country to see it. In spite of _____,
the tourists have been picking leaves and cutting their names on the
tree-trunk. So far, not one of them has been _____
_____!

Secondly retell the story in the third person.

Ⅳ Active questions

1. What is the name of the tiny village?
2. Why the number of visitors to the village has increased?
3. When was the tree planted?
4. What will happen if anyone touches the tree?
5. What did many villagers believe?
6. What did the vicar point out?
7. What have the tourists been doing in spite of all that has been said?
8. Has anyone been struck down by sudden death?

Lesson 59

In or out?

进来还是出去？

I Use the word(s) to make sentence(s)

Pay

_____ .

Pay — bill

_____ .

Pay — bill — dinner

_____ .

Comfortable

_____ .

Comfortable — stay

_____ .

Comfortable — stay — own country

_____ .

Succeed

_____ .

Succeed — survive

_____ .

Succeed — survive — training

_____ .

II Practice the key patterns

T: collect stamps — swim in a small river

S1: When I was young, I used to collect stamps. What about you?

S2: I used to swim in a small river.

Practice: (1) write to a pen pal — play with my cousin

(2) raise two golden fish — raise a kitty

(3) watch animation a lot — play computer games

(4) read many Chinese poems — read many novels

T: do my homework

S1: What were you doing at eight last night?

S2: I was doing my homework in the study.

Practice: (1) wash my clothes

(2) prepare materials for the report

(3) shop in a supermarket

(4) have a bathing

T: delayed by heavy traffic

S1: I have been waiting for you for two hours. Where have you been?

S2: I am very sorry. I was delayed by heavy traffic.

Practice: (1) stopped by a heavy rain

(2) caught in a storm

(3) involved in an accident

(4) delayed by the meeting

III Retell the story

Firstly complete the blanks and remember what you said.

Our dog, Rex, used to _____ and bark.

Every time he wanted to come into the garden he would _____

_____ . As the neighbors _____ , my husband spent weeks training him to _____

_____ . Rex soon became an expert at opening the gate. However, when I was _____ last week, I noticed him in the garden near the gate. This time he was barking so that someone would let him out! Since then, he has _____ . As soon as he opens the gate from the outside, he _____

_____ until the gate shuts. Then he sits and barks until someone lets him out. After this he immediately lets himself in and begins barking again. Yesterday my husband _____ and Rex got so _____ .

Secondly retell the story in the third person.

Ⅳ Active questions

1. What is the name of our dog?
2. What did he use to do?
3. What did the neighbor complain of?
4. What did my husband train him to do?
5. Last week what did I notice?
6. This time why he was barking?
7. What kind of bad habit did he develop?
8. What did my husband do yesterday?

Lesson 60

The future

卜算未来

I Use the word (s) to make sentence (s)

Remove

_____.

Remove — dish

_____.

Remove — dish — table

_____.

Develop

_____.

Develop — habit

_____.

Develop — habit — smoking

_____.

Increase

_____.

Increase — income

_____.

Increase — income — hard

_____.

II Practice the key patterns

T: tell her about the party — I see her

S1: Have you told her about the party?

S2: Not yet. I will tell her about the party the moment I see her.

Practice: (1) inform him of the meeting — I am off work

(2) give Mark a phone call — I am free

(3) invite your friends to your home — everything is done

(4) hold a birthday party for your wife — I have much free time

T: come — half an hour

S1: Will your brother coming soon?

S2: Yes. He will be here in about half an hour.

Practice: (1) arrive — an hour

(2) return — two days

(3) get back — a week

(4) come back — several days

T: live — since I was born

S1: How long have you been living in this place?

S2: I have been living here since I was born.

Practice: (1) work — since last April

(2) study — since 2004

(3) married — for 20 years

(4) doing research on dinosaur — since I graduate from college

III Retell the story

Firstly complete the blanks and remember what you said.

At a village fair, I decided to _____ called Madam

Bellinsky. I went into her tent and she told me to sit down. After I had _____, she _____ and said: 'A relation of yours is coming to see you. She will be arriving this evening and _____. The moment you leave this tent, you will _____. A woman you know well will _____. She will speak to you and then she will _____. That is all.' As soon as I went outside, I forgot all about Madam Bellinsky because my wife hurried towards me. 'Where have you been hiding?' she asked _____. 'Your sister will be here in less than an hour and we must be _____. We are late already.' As she walked away, I _____.

Secondly retell the story in the third person.

IV Active questions

1. What did I decide to do at a village fair?

2. What did I give her?

3. What did she do before she told me something about my future?

4. According to what she said, who was going to see me?

5. When would I get a big surprise?

6. Why did I forget all about the fortune — teller after I went outside?

7. In fact, who is going to see me?

8. Where would my wife and I meet the coming visitor?

V Fill the blanks with the correct form of the verbs given

1. Do you intend _____ (tell) him about this incident?

2. Never expect my lost pen to _____ (find).

3. The next day, the child was _____ (take) to his father's workplace.

4. Usually I _____ （get） up at seven o'clock every morning.

5. I have finished _____ （make） a plan for the project.

6. Tom prefers _____ （stay） at his grandma's house than his own.

7. When I got home, my sister told me that she _____ （lose） her watch.

8. Unfortunately, I failed _____ （pass） the math exam.

Trouble with the Hubble
哈勃望远镜的困境

I Use the word (s) to make sentence (s)

Enjoy

_____.

Enjoy — try

_____.

Enjoy — try — different

_____.

Claim

_____.

Claim — personal

_____.

Claim — personal — possession

_____.

Catch

_____.

Catch — train

_____.

Catch — train — join

_____.

II Practice the key patterns

T: work in the law office

S1: Will you still be working in the law office in a year's time?

S2: Yes. By that time I have been working in the law office for three
    years.

Practice: (1) live in this town

(2) study this topic

(3) collect model planes

(4) work with that guy

T: a heavy rain — take an umbrella

S1: The radio says that there will be a heavy rain this evening.

S2: In that case, you'd better take an umbrella with you.

Practice: (1) heavy fog — get back home earlier

(2) be very cold — put on more clothes

(3) big snow — not drive your car to work

(4) be hot — take the sunglass with you

T: repair the gate

S1: The gate is being repaired now.

S2: Oh. I thought it was repaired last month.

Practice: (1) water the garden

(2) feed the chickens

(3) iron the clothes

(4) clean the bedroom

III Retell the story

Firstly complete the blanks and remember what you said.

The Hubble telescope was _____ by NASA on April
20, 1990 at a cost of over a billion dollars. Right from the start ____

_____ the Hubble. The pictures it sent us were very disappointing because _____! NASA is now going to put the telescope right, so it will soon be _____

_____ to repair it. The shuttle Endeavour will be _____

_____ to the Hubble. A robot-arm from the Endeavour will grab the telescope and hold it while the astronauts _____

_____. Of course, the Hubble is _____

_____, so it will soon be sending us _____

_____ that we have ever seen. The Hubble will tell us _____

_____ the age and size of the universe. By the time you read this, the Hubble's eagle eye will have sent us thousands and thousands of _____.

Secondly retell the story in the third person.

IV Active questions

1. Who sent the Hubble telescope into space?
2. When was the Hubble sent into space?
3. Why the pictures it sent us were disappointing?
4. What is NASA now going to do?
5. What is the name of the shuttle?
6. What will the telescope send to us?
7. What will the Hubble tell us?
8. Are the pictures the Hubble will send us wonderful?

After the fire

大火之后

I Use the word (s) to make sentence (s)

Struggle

_____ .

Struggle — control

_____ .

Struggle — control — temper

_____ .

Threaten

_____ .

Threaten — kill

_____ .

Threaten — kill — family

_____ .

Expert

_____ .

Expert — handle

_____ .

Expert — handle — affair

_____ .

II Practice the key patterns

T: get this job — study in England

S1: What had he been doing before he got this job?

S2: Before he got this job, he had been studying in England.

Practice: (1) move to this place — work as an engineer

(2) decide to go abroad — travel all over China

(3) enter this company — work in a food company

(4) purchase his master's degree — teach English in a mountain area

T: write love stories — work in a newspaper office

S1: Does Susan still write love stories?

S2: She wrote love stories two years ago. Now she works in a newspaper office.

Practice: (1) sell books — work in a commercial museum

(2) make shoes — work in a shoe shop of his own

(3) act in plays — write plays for the film company

(4) work as a cook — be a manager of a big restaurant

T: attend the conference — have time

S1: Will you attend the conference tomorrow?

S2: I would attend the conference if I had time.

Practice: (1) join the birthday party — be free

(2) take a trip to Hangzhou — have enough money

(3) study abroad — get a full scholarship

(4) buy a new car — get promoted

III Retell the story

Firstly complete the blanks and remember what you said.

Firemen had been _____ for nearly three

weeks before they could _____ . A short time
before, great trees had covered the countryside for miles around.
Now, smoke still _____ over the desolate
hills. Winter was coming on and the hills _____
_____ , for heavy rain would not only wash away the soil but would
_____ as well. When the fire had at last
been put out, the forest authorities _____
which would grow quickly. The seed was _____
_____ by aero planes. The planes had been _____
_____ when it began to rain. By then, however, in many places
the grass had already _____ . In place of the great trees
which had been growing there for centuries, patches of green had
begun to _____ .
Secondly retell the story in the third person.

Ⅳ Active questions

1. How long had the firefighters been fighting the fire?
2. What was the countryside like a short time before?
3. What was the countryside like now?
4. Why the hills threatened the surrounding villages with destruction?
5. What did the forest authorities order?
6. How was the seed sprayed over the ground?
7. When did it begin to rain?
8. What had begun to appear in the blackened soil?

Lesson

63 She was not amused
她并不觉得好笑

I Use the word (s) to make sentence (s)

Prepare

_____.

Prepare — meal

_____.

Prepare — meal — daughter

_____.

Follow

_____.

Follow — rule

_____.

Follow — rule — school

_____.

Admire

_____.

Admire — courage

_____.

Admire — courage — ask

_____.

II Practice the key patterns

T: take this job

S1: Her father suggested that she should take this job.

S2: She'd better take her father's advice.

Practice: (1) study abroad

(2) continue to write poems

(3) work in an transnational cooperation

(4) accept the invitation

T: go to the concert — busy with my work

S1: Will you go to the concert with us?

S2: Sorry. I am busy with my work right now.

Practice: (1) go to the entertainment park — prepare for the exam

(2) watch Shakespeare's play — clean the house

(3) visit the exhibition — see the dentist

T: lose your watch — wait in a long queue

S1: When did you lose your watch?

S2: I lost my watch as I was waiting in a long queue.

Practice: (1) drop the wallet — wait for the bus at the station

(2) see my English teacher — step onto the bus

(3) catch sight of my missing cat — pass the neighbor's house

III Retell the story

Firstly complete the blanks and remember what you said.

Jeremy Hampden has ＿＿＿＿＿＿＿＿＿＿＿＿＿＿＿ and is very popular at parties. Everybody admires him for ＿＿＿＿＿＿＿＿

＿＿＿＿ — everybody, that is, except his six-year-old daughter, Jenny. Recently, one of Jeremy's closest friends asked him to ＿＿＿＿

_____. This is the sort of thing that Jeremy loves. He prepared the speech carefully and went to the wedding with Jenny. He had included _____ and, of course, it was a great success. As soon as he had finished, Jenny told him she wanted to go home. Jeremy was _____ but he did as his daughter asked. On the way home, he asked Jenny if she had _____. To his surprise, she said she hadn't. Jeremy asked her _____ and she told him that she did not like to _____!

Secondly retell the story in the third person.

IV Active questions

1. What does everybody admires Jeremy for?
2. How old is Jenny?
3. What did one of Jeremy's friends ask him to do?
4. Does Jeremy like this sort of thing?
5. What was included in the speech?
6. Was it a great success?
7. What did Jeremy feel after hearing that Jenny wanted to go home?
8. Why didn't Jenny enjoy the speech?

V Translate the following sentences into English

1. 到今天晚上我就会完成那个项目了。
2. 如果明天天气好，我们去野餐吧。
3. 即使我劝他，他也不会听我的。
4. 我们原本以为这是一次惊奇的旅行。
5. 出国前他游玩了很多国内的名胜。
6. 这几天他一直在忙那个项目。

7. 我小时候常常看动画片。
8. 据说她现在在美国一所著名大学读书。
9. 你知道这件事是怎么发生的吗？
10. 他的爷爷建议他去一家大公司工作。

Lesson
64
The Channel Tunnel
海峡隧道

I Use the word (s) to make sentence (s)

Strict

_____.

Strict — work

_____.

Strict — work — outstanding

_____.

Design

_____.

Design — fantastic

_____.

Design — fantastic — attract

_____.

Embarrass

_____.

Embarrass — find

_____.

Embarrass — find — mistake

_____.

Ⅱ Practice the key patterns

T: break her leg — be more careful

S1: I heard that she broke her leg.

S2: Yes. If she had been more careful, she wouldn't have broken her leg.

Practice: (1) fail the exam — study harder

(2) fail to catch the bus — get up earlier

(3) miss the plane — arrive earlier

(4) get fired — be more diligent

T: go to the theatre

S1: Did you go to the theatre with them?

S2: Yes. Because Mike insisted that I should go with them.

Practice: (1) go to the theme park

(2) watch the volleyball match

(3) climb up the mountain

(4) visit the Imperial Palace

T: hand in her report

S1: Has Sarah handed in her report?

S2: Yes, she has. She handed it in this morning.

Practice: (1) deliver the parcel

(2) inform you of the meeting

(3) telephone her parents

(4) send the gift to her grandma

Ⅲ Retell the story

Firstly complete the blanks and remember what you said.

In 1858, a _____, Aime Thome de Gamond, arrived in England with a plan for a _____.

He said that it would be possible to _____ of
the Channel. This platform would _____ . The
tunnel would be well — ventilated if tall chimneys were built above
sea level. In 1860, a better plan was _____ by an
Englishman, William Low. He suggested that a double railway-
tunnel should be built. This would _____ , for
if a train entered this tunnel, it would _____
behind it. Forty-two years later a tunnel was actually begun. If, at
the time, the British had not _____ , it would have
been completed. The world had to wait almost another 100 years for
the Channel Tunnel. It was _____ on March 7,
1994, finally connecting Britain to the European continent.

Secondly retell the story in the third person.

Ⅳ Active questions

1. Where did Aime come from?
2. With what did Aime arrive in England?
3. What would be possible according to Aime?
4. What would this platform serve as?
5. What did Aime suggest?
6. Why would a double railway-tunnel solve the problem of
   ventilation?
7. When was the tunnel actually begun?
8. When was the Channel Tunnel officially opened?

Jumbo versus the police
小象对警察

I Use the word (s) to make sentence (s)

Refuse

_____ .

Refuse — accept

_____ .

Refuse — accept — invitation

_____ .

Eager

_____ .

Eager — win

_____ .

Eager — win — the first prize

_____ .

Threaten

_____ .

Threaten — kill

_____ .

Threaten — kill — son

_____ .

II Practice the key patterns

T: get up early — be late for work

S1: So you mean that I have to get up early.

S2: Yes. Otherwise, you'll be late for work.

Practice: (1) see the doctor — be sick more seriously

(2) attend the ceremony — be fired

(3) hand in the thesis — fail the course

(4) cite this document — get a low score

T: buy the red skirt

S1: You should have bought the red skirt.

S2: Yes. I knew. But I just prefer the white one.

Practice: (1) go there next Monday

(2) travel to Macao

(3) rent the cheap house

(4) drive slowly

T: put away the clothes

S1: It is raining now. My clothes are still hanging outside.

S2: Oh. You should have put them away this morning.

Practice: (1) water the flowers in the garden

(2) lay the table

(3) take her advice

(4) go over the lessons very hard

III Retell the story

Firstly complete the blanks and remember what you said.

Last Christmas, the circus owner, Jimmy Gates, decided to __

_____ to a children's hospital. _____ as Father

Christmas and accompanied by a 'guard of honor' of six pretty girls,

he _____ a baby elephant called Jumbo.
He should have known that _____. A
policeman _____ Jimmy and told him he ought to have gone along
a side street as Jumbo was _____. Though Jimmy
agreed to go at once, Jumbo _____. Fifteen policemen
had to push very hard to _____. The police had a
difficult time, but they were most amused. 'Jumbo must weigh a few
tons,' said a policeman afterwards, 'so it was fortunate that we
didn't _____. Of course, we should arrest him,
but as he _____, we shall let him off this time.'
Secondly retell the story in the third person.

IV Active questions

1. What was the name of the circus owner?
2. What did he decide to do?
3. What did he dress up as?
4. What did he ride when he set off?
5. What should he have known?
6. What did the policeman tell him?
7. How many policemen had to push him?
8. What did a policeman say afterwards?

Sweet as honey!

像蜜一样甜！

I Use the word (s) to make sentence (s)

Accompany

_____.

Accompany — friend

_____.

Accompany — friend — film

_____.

Rescue

_____.

Rescue — little girl

_____.

Rescue — little girl — fire

_____.

Fear

_____.

Fear — stay

_____.

Fear — stay — alone

_____.

II　Practice the key patterns

T: go to the tailor's — have my pants cut short

S1: Where are you going?

S2: I am going to the tailor's. I want to have my pants cut short.

Practice: (1) go to the barber's — have my hair cut

(2) go to do some laundry — have my clothes washed

(3) go to the dentist — have my teeth cleaned

T: receive a short message

S1: Where is Sam now?

S2: I don't know. He left a moment ago after he had received a short message.

Practice: (1) receive a phone call

(2) have a talk with the manager

(3) have a fight with his colleague

(4) discuss with the group members

T: watch the movie — three times

S1: Will you watch the movie with me?

S2: Sorry. I have watched this movie three times.

Practice: (1) visit 798 art museum — four times

(2) do another experiment — do five experiments already

(3) take some photos — take hundreds of photos this week

(4) see grandparents — three times

III　Retell the story

Firstly complete the blanks and remember what you said.

In 1963 a Lancaster bomber _____, a remote place in the South Pacific, a long way west of Samoa. The plane wasn't _____, but over the years, the crash was

forgotten and the wreck _____. Then in 1989, ___
_____ after the crash, the plane was _____
in an _____ of the island. By this time, a Lancaster
bomber in reasonable condition was _____.
The French authorities had the plane packaged and moved in parts
back to France. Now a group of enthusiasts are going to _____
_____. It has four Rolls-royce Merlin engines, but the group
will need to have only three of them rebuilt. Imagine their _____
_____ when they broke open the packing cases and found
that the fourth engine was sweet as honey — still _____
_____. A colony of bees had turned the engine into a hive and it was
_____ in beeswax!
Secondly retell the story in the third person.

IV Active questions

1. Where did the bomber crash in 1963?
2. Was the plane badly damaged?
3. How many years later the plane was rediscovered?
4. How did the French authorities deal with the plane?
5. What are a group of the enthusiasts going to do?
6. How many engines does the plane have?
7. What did the enthusiasts feel when they find the fourth engine?
8. What happened to the fourth engine?

V Please make up a story based on the following beginning

You are in a railway station. It is becoming dark. But there's no
money left in your pocket. Then an idea occurs to you _____.

I Use the word (s) to make sentence (s)

Remote

_____ .

Remote — place

_____ .

Remote — place — live

_____ .

Imagine

_____ .

Imagine — feel

_____ .

Imagine — feel — first prize

_____ .

Sympathetic

_____ .

Sympathetic — homeless

_____ .

Sympathetic — homeless — children

II Practice the key patterns

T: do my experiment

S1: What were you doing this afternoon? Mr. Smith came and wanted to talk to you.

S2: I was doing my experiment in the lab at that moment.

Practice: (1) wash my clothes

(2) see the dentist

(3) shop in the shopping mall

(4) read in the library

T: post the letter

S1: Has Tim posted the letter?

S2: Not yet. But he will post it this afternoon.

Practice: (1) check the experiment result

(2) clean the kitchen

(3) make a plan of the summer holiday

(4) wash the car

T: smoke here — smoke in the smoking room

S1: Would you mind my smoking here?

S2: You'd better smoke in the smoking room.

Practice: (1) open the window — open the door

(2) sit here — take the next seat

(3) hang my coat here — hang it there

III Retell the story

Firstly complete the blanks and remember what you said.

Haroun Tazieff, the Polish scientist, has spent _____

_____ active volcanoes and deep caves in all parts of the world. In 1948, he went to Lake Kivu in the Congo to _____ .

which he later named Kituro. Tazieff was able to _____

_____ while it was _____ . Though he managed

to _____ , he could not stay near the volcano

for very long. He noticed that a river of liquid rock was coming

towards him. It _____ , but Tazieff managed

to _____ . He waited until the volcano became

quiet and he was able to return two days later. This time, he

managed to _____ of Kituro so that he could take

photographs and _____ . Tazieff has often _____

_____ in this way. He has been able to tell us more about

active volcanoes than any man alive.

Secondly retell the story in the third person.

IV Active questions

1. Where did Tazieff come from?
2. What has he spend his lifetime doing?
3. When did he go to Lake Kivu?
4. What was he able to do?
5. What did he manage to do?
6. Could he stay near the volcano for very long?
7. What did he notice?
8. When was he able to return?
9. Why did he climb into the mouth of Kituro?
10. What has Tazieff often done?

Lesson 68

Persistent

纠缠不休

I *Use the word (s) to make sentence (s)*

Active

_____.

Active — collect

_____.

Active — collect — plane models

_____.

Escape

_____.

Escape — building

_____.

Escape — building — fire

_____.

Risk

_____.

Risk — life

_____.

Risk — life — study

_____.

II　Practice the key patterns

T: sweep the floor

S1: What were you doing when it started to rain?

S2: I was sweeping the floor. What's the matter?

Practice: (1) pack my belongings

(2) do crosswords

(3) look after the baby

(4) learn Japanese in the study

T: Tom — four years

S1: When did you meet Tom?

S2: Last Tuesday. I had not seen him for almost four years.

Practice: (1) Jennifer — three years

(2) Sophia — seven months

(3) Samson — about one year

(4) David — about one semester

T: the dentist's — sit in the waiting room

S1: Where have you been?

S2: In the dentist's. I have been sitting in the waiting room for the whole morning.

Practice: (1) the head teacher's office — talk with him

(2) the gym — do exercise

(3) the office — compile a guide book

(4) the music hall — listen to classic music

III　Retell the story

Firstly complete the blanks and remember what you said.

I crossed the street to _____, but he saw me and came running towards me. It was no use _____, so

I waved to him. I never _____ Nigel Dykes. He never has
anything to do. No matter how busy you are, he always _____
_____. I had to think of a way of preventing him from _____
_____.

'Hello, Nigel,' I said. 'Fancy _____!'

'Hi, Elizabeth,' Bert answered. 'I was just wondering how to
_____ — until I saw you. You're not busy doing anything,
are you?'

'No, not at all,' I answered. 'I'm going to'

'Would you _____ with you?' he asked, before I
had _____.

'Not at all,' I lied, 'but I'm going to _____.'

'Then I'll come with you,' he answered. 'There's always _____
_____ in the waiting room!'

Secondly retell the story in the third person.

Ⅳ Active questions

1. Why did I cross the street?

2. Do I enjoy meeting Nigel?

3. What does he insist on doing all the time?

4. What did I have to do this time?

5. What was Nigel wondering?

6. What did he ask before I had finished speaking?

7. What was I going to do this morning?

8. What would he do while I was seeing the dentist?

Lesson 69

But not murder!
并非谋杀！

I Use the word(s) to make sentence(s)

Avoid

_____ .

Avoid — meet

_____ .

Avoid — meet — talkative guy

_____ .

Prevent

_____ .

Prevent — lose

_____ .

Prevent — lose — contest

_____ .

Rude

_____ .

Rude — remark

_____ .

Rude — remark — privacy

_____ .

Ⅱ Practice the key patterns

T: happy — pass the English final exam

S1: What has happened to Lisa? She looks so happy.

S2: She must have passed the English final exam.

Practice: (1) sad — be dumped by his girlfriend

(2) tired — work the whole day

(3) puzzled — come across a hard problem

(4) upset — be scolded by the teacher

T: ask — some details on this issue

S1: Could I ask you something about the details on this issue?

S2: No! I was being asked about the details on this issue the whole morning.

Practice: (1) interview — your latest released book

(2) consult — the latest development of this program

(3) ask — the sales figure of last month

T: finish writing the novel — next week

S1: Can you finish writing the novel on time?

S2: Yes. I will have finished writing it by next week.

Practice: (1) complete your thesis — next month

(2) hand in your term paper — this Friday

(3) find a solution to this problem — next

(4) finish painting the room — this June

Ⅲ Retell the story

Firstly complete the blanks and remember what you said.

I was being tested for _____. I had been asked to drive in _____. After having been instructed to drive out of town, I began to _____.

Sure that I had passed, I was almost beginning to _____

_____. The examiner must have been _____, for he

smiled and said, 'Just one more thing, Mr. Eames. Let us suppose

that a child suddenly crosses the road in front of you. As soon as I __

_____, you must stop within five feet.' I continued

driving and after some time, the examiner tapped loudly. Though the

sound could be heard clearly, it _____. I

suddenly pressed the brake pedal hard and we were both _____

_____. The examiner looked at me sadly. 'Mr. Eames,' he

said, in a _____, 'you have just killed that

child!'

Secondly retell the story in the third person.

Ⅳ Active questions

1. What was I being tested for?

2. What did I have been asked to do?

3. When did I begin to acquire confidence?

4. Why did the examiner smile?

5. What should I do as soon as the examiner taps on the window?

6. Did I react very quickly?

7. What did I do then?

8. What did the examiner say to me at last?

Ⅴ Fill the blanks with the correct form of the verbs given

1. Her brother is supposed _____ during the World War Ⅱ.
   (kill)

2. After _____ a Grammy in 2003, she went abroad. (award)

3. If there _____ no rain, we would have arrived the spot.
   (be)

4. The headmaster suggests that everyone _____ a cap on that day. (wear)

5. I never regret _____ for you for such a long time. (wait)

6. I was _____ learn that they had been married for half a year. (surprise)

7. She enjoys herself _____ various kinds of stamps. (collect)

8. He must _____ the test for a driving license. (pass)

9. You'd better _____ on more clothes because it is cold outside. (put)

10. These days I am busy _____ a collection of short stories. (edit)

Lesson 70

Red for danger
危险的红色

I Use the word (s) to make sentence (s)

Mind

_____

Mind — icy

_____

Mind — icy — school

_____

Throw

_____

Throw — old

_____

Throw — old — newspaper

_____

Cross

_____

Cross — room

_____

Cross — room — meet

_____

II Practice the key patterns

T: not show up at the party — get a bad cold

S1: I wonder why he didn't show up at the party.

S2: Alice told me that he had got a bad cold.

Practice: (1) be late for work — be involved in an accident

(2) miss the bus — get up too late

(3) agree with the plan — find it was a plan of some merit

T: come to class

S1: Has Kate come to class?

S2: No, she hasn't. But she said she would come.

Practice: (1) attend the lecture

(2) buy a car

(3) water the flowers

(4) finalize the design

T: finish the term paper

S1: How long did it take you to finish the term paper?

S2: It took me two hours to finish it.

Practice: (1) drive from Beijing to Tianjin

(2) cook the meal

(3) visit the museum

(4) make your bed

III Retell the story

Firstly complete the blanks and remember what you said.

During a bullfight, a drunk suddenly _____

_____. The crowd began to shout, but the drunk was _____

_____. The bull was busy with the matador at the time, but it

suddenly _____ who was _____

_____. Apparently sensitive to criticism, the bull forgot all about the matador and _____. The crowd suddenly grew quiet. The drunk, however, seemed _____. When the bull got close to him, he _____. The crowd broke into cheers and the drunk bowed. By this time, however, three men had come into the ring and they quickly _____ ____. Even the bull seemed to feel sorry for him, for it _____ _____ until the drunk was out of the way before once more _____ the matador.

Secondly retell the story in the third person.

Ⅳ Active questions

1. What did the drunk do during a bullfight?
2. What did the crowd begin to do?
3. What was the drunk doing while the bull caught sight of him?
4. What was the bull sensitive to?
5. What did the drunk do when the bull got close to him?
6. What did the drunk react to the crowd's cheers?
7. How many men had come into the ring?
8. Why did the bull seem to be sympathetic with the drunk?

A famous clock
一个著名的大钟

I Use the word(s) to make sentence(s)

Aware

_____.

Aware — danger

_____.

Aware — danger — face

_____.

Hurry

_____.

Hurry — air port

_____.

Hurry — air port — meet

_____.

Acquire

_____.

Acquire — knowledge

_____.

Acquire — knowledge — university

_____.

II Practice the key patterns

T: return from the holiday

S1: When will return from the holiday?

S2: I will return in a month.

Practice: (1) write the fiction

(2) buy the English magazine

(3) visit your professor

(4) bake the bread

T: on the way home — go home earlier

S1: It starts to rain now. Nora is still on the way home.

S2: Oh. She should have gone home earlier.

Practice: (1) on the way to the station — start earlier

(2) on the way to school — get up earlier

(3) on the way to the hospital — go to see the doctor yesterday

T: help — succeed

S1: You finally make it.

S2: Yes. Without your help, I would not have succeeded.

Practice: (1) encouragement — win the first prize

(2) support — complete the paper

(3) aid — join that international company

III Retell the story

Firstly complete the blanks and remember what you said.

When you visit London, one of the first things you will see is Big Ben, the famous clock which can be _____ on the B. B. C. If the Houses of Parliament _____ in 1834, the great clock would never have been erected. Big Ben takes

its name from Sir Benjamin Hall who was _____
when the new Houses of Parliament were being built. It is not only of
immense size, but is _____ as well. Officials from
Greenwich Observatory have _____. On the
B. B. C. you can _____ because microphones are
connected to the clock tower. Big Ben has rarely _____.
Once, however, it _____. A painter who had been
working on the tower _____ on one of the hands
and slowed it down!

Secondly retell the story in the third person.

IV Active questions

1. What is one of the first things you will see when visiting London?
2. Why was Big Ben erected?
3. Where does the Big Ben get its name?
4. What was Sir Benjamin responsible for?
5. Who have the clock checked?
6. How often would they check the clock?
7. Why you can hear the clock when it is actually striking on the
   B. B. C. ?
8. Why once did the clock go wrong?

Lesson 72

A car called *Bluebird*

"蓝鸟"汽车

I Use the word (s) to make sentence (s)

Check

_____ .

Check — door

_____ .

Check — door — every night

_____ .

Damage

_____ .

Damage — building

_____ .

Damage — building — earthquake

_____ .

Glance

_____ .

Glance — painting

_____ .

Glance — painting — wall

_____ .

II Practice the key patterns

T: able to — deal with complex interpersonal relations

S1: What do you think of Julia?

S2: She is able to deal with complex interpersonal relations.

Practice: (1) qualified at — calculate big numbers

(2) capable of — collect rare materials

(3) good at — type words

(4) efficient at — solve difficult problems

T: rain for two hours — this afternoon

S1: How long has it been raining?

S2: It has been raining for two hours. It began to rain this afternoon.

Practice: (1) teach English for ten years — when I graduated from college

(2) study in the U. S. A. for three years — when I was 19

(3) work in the research institute for two years — after moving to this city

(4) read English newspaper — this early morning

T: visit the museum

S1: Is it your first time to visit the museum?

S2: No, I have visited the museum several times.

Practice: (1) go to Disneyland

(2) visit the Military Museum

(3) join a club

(4) have a blind date

III Retell the story

Firstly complete the blanks and remember what you said.

The _____, Sir Malcolm Campbell, was the

first man to drive at over 300 miles per hour. He set up _____

_____ in September 1935 at Bonneville Salt Flats, Utah.

Bluebird, the car he was driving, had been _____ for him.

It was _____ and had a 2500-horsepower engine.

Although Campbell reached a speed of over 304 miles per hour, he

had _____ because a tyre burst during the first

run. After his attempt, Campbell was _____ that his

average speed had been 299 miles per hour. However, a few days

later, he was told that _____. His average speed

had been 301 miles per hour. Since that time, racing drivers have

reached speeds of over 600 miles an hour. Following _____

_____ many years later, Sir Malcolm's son, Donald, also set up

a world record. Like his father, he was driving a car called *Bluebird*.

Secondly retell the story in the third person.

IV Active questions

1. Who was Sir Malcolm Campbell?

2. When did he set up a new world record?

3. What was the name of the car he was driving?

4. How long was the car?

5. Why did Campbell have difficulty in controlling the car?

6. What was he disappointed to learn?

7. In fact, what was his real average speed?

8. What was the name of Sir Campbell's son?

V Translate the following sentences into English

1. 月球上没有生命。

2. 很遗憾，你没有被录取。

3. 在去澳洲读书前，他游览了很多地方。

4. 大家都认为学好英语很重要。

5. 我永远都不会忘记你给我的帮助。

6. 一定是史密斯放火烧了那座房子。

7. 他常常偷懒，所以被炒鱿鱼了。

8. 面试时，他紧张得不停地冒汗。

9. 我们能做的就是赶快回家。

10. 我们惊奇地发现他们竟是父子。

Lesson 73

The record-holder
记录保持者

I Use the word (s) to make sentence (s)

Reveal

_____ .

Reveal — happiness

_____ .

Reveal — happiness — scholarship

_____ .

Guilty

_____ .

Guilty — lie

_____ .

Guilty — lie — score

_____ .

Prefer

_____ .

Prefer — stay

_____ .

Prefer — stay — go abroad

_____ .

II Practice the key patterns

T: good at swimming — win a first prize in a swimming competition

S1: People say that he is good at swimming.

S2: Yes. It is said that he once won the first prize in a swimming competition.

Practice: (1) clever — win a full scholarship from the university

(2) lazy — never clean his own room

(3) careful — check the homework three twice before handing it in

T: a teacher — teach math

S1: How long have you been a teacher?

S2: I have been teaching math for four years.

Practice: (1) baby — sitter — look after babies

(2) poet — write poems

(3) architect — design houses

(4) barber — cut hair

T: hand in the paper

S1: You should have handed in your paper yesterday.

S2: Sorry. I totally forgot about it.

Practice: (1) mend the curtain

(2) throw away the rubbish

(3) paint the dining room

(4) recite that passage

III Retell the story

Firstly complete the blanks and remember what you said.

Children who _____ are unimaginative. A quiet day's fishing, or eight hours in a cinema _____

_____ , is usually as far as they get. They have all been _____

_____ by a boy who, while playing truant, traveled 1600 miles. He

hitchhiked to Dover and, towards evening, went into a boat to

_____. When he woke up next morning, he discovered

that the boat had, in the meantime, traveled to Calais. No one

noticed the boy as he _____. From there, he hitchhiked to

Paris in a lorry. The driver gave him a few biscuits and a cup of

coffee and _____. The next car the boy stopped

did not take him into the centre of Paris as he hoped it would, but to

Perpignan on the French-Spanish border. There he was _____

_____ and sent back to England by the _____. He

has surely _____   the thousands of children who

_____.

Secondly retell the story in the third person.

Ⅳ Active questions

1. Which children are unimaginative?
2. What would they usually do when they play truant?
3. How far did the boy travel when he played truant?
4. How did he go to Dover?
5. What did he discover when he woke up next morning?
6. What did the driver give him?
7. Where did the next car take him to?
8. Who sent him back to England?

Lesson 74

Out of the limelight

舞台之外

I Use the word (s) to make sentence (s)

Astonished

_____ .

Astonished — find

_____ .

Astonished — find — steal

_____ .

Fortunate

_____ .

Fortunate — escape

_____ .

Fortunate — escape — unhurt

_____ .

Approach

_____ .

Approach — inform

_____ .

Approach — inform — conference

_____ .

II Practice the key patterns

T: work in England

S1: She went to work in England last year.

S2: Is she still working there?

Practice: (1) study in Sydney

(2) move to the west region

(3) enter a famous company

(4) join the club

T: post the letter

S1: Did you post the letter yesterday.

S2: Sorry, I didn't. I will post it right away.

Practice: (1) do the laundry

(2) check E-mail box

(3) send the report to the teacher

(4) return my book

T: feed the dog — no dog food left

S1: You should have fed the dog.

S2: But there is no dog food left.

Practice: (1) throw away the garbage — no dustbin nearby

(2) iron the clothes — no iron found

(3) clean the floor — no broom

III Retell the story

Firstly complete the blanks and remember what you said.

An ancient bus stopped by a dry river bed and _____

_____ got off. Dressed in _____, they had

taken _____ so that no one should recognize them.

But as they soon discovered, disguises can sometimes be _____

_____ .

'This is _____ ,' said Gloria Gleam.

'It couldn't be better, Gloria,' Brinksley Meers agreed. 'No newspaper men, no film fans! Why don't we come more often?'

Meanwhile, two other actors, Rockwall Slinger and Merlin Greeves, had carried two large food baskets to _____

__ . When they had all made themselves comfortable, a stranger appeared. He looked _____ . 'Now you get out of here, all of you!' he shouted. 'I'm sheriff here. Do you see that notice? It says "No Camping" — in case you can't read!'

'Look, sheriff,' said Rockwall, 'don't be _____

_____ . I'm Rockwall Slinger and this is Merlin Greeves. '

'Oh, is it?' said the sheriff _____ . 'Well, I'm Brinksley Meers, and my other name is Gloria Gleam. Now you get out of here fast!'

Secondly retell the story in the third person.

IV Active questions

1. Who got off an ancient bus?
2. What were they dressed in?
3. Why did they take special precautions?
4. What did Gloria Gleam say?
5. What did two other actors do meanwhile?
6. How did the stranger look?
7. What did Rockwall say?
8. What did the sheriff say with a sneer?

Lesson
75 SOS

呼救信号

I Use the word(s) to make sentence(s)

Manage

_____.

Manage — get

_____.

Manage — get — in time

_____.

Sensitive

_____.

Sensitive — figure

_____.

Sensitive — figure — eat less

_____.

Authority

_____.

Authority — order

_____.

Authority — order — return

_____.

II Practice the key patterns

T: search material for my thesis

S1: What have been doing the whole morning? I couldn't find you.

S2: I have been searching for materials for my thesis.

Practice: (1) decorate the wedding car

(2) make meat pies

(3) pick apples in the orchard

(4) pack up the parcel

T: show — great

S1: What do you think of the show yesterday?

S2: It was great. I love it!

Practice: (1) performance — wonderful

(2) movie — touching

(3) exhibition — gorgeous

(4) concert — spectacular

T: this Friday — work on my paper

S1: Are you free this Friday?

S2: No. This Friday I will be working on my paper.

Practice: (1) tomorrow aftenoon — write my composition

(2) tonight — discuss with Sally about the homework

(3) next Monday — listen to a lecture

III Retell the story

Firstly complete the blanks and remember what you said.

When a light passenger plane _____ some time ago, it crashed in the mountains and its pilot was killed. The only passengers, a young woman and her two baby daughters, were ____ ____. It was the middle of winter. Snow lay thick on the ground.

The woman knew that _____. When it grew dark, she _____ and put the children inside it, covering them with all the clothes she could find. During the night, it _____. The woman kept as near as she could to the children and even tried to get into the case herself, but it was too small. Early next morning she heard planes passing overhead and wondered how she could _____. Then she had an idea. She stamped out the letters 'SOS' in the snow. Fortunately, a pilot saw the signal and sent a message by radio to the nearest town. It was not long before _____ on the scene to _____ of the plane crash.

Secondly retell the story in the third person.

Ⅳ Active questions

1. Where did the plane crash?
2. Who was killed?
3. Who were the only passengers?
4. What was the weather like at that time?
5. What did she do in order to keep the babies from cold?
6. How did she make the letters "SOS"?
7. How did the pilot send the message to the nearest town?
8. Who arrived to rescue the woman and two babies?

Ⅴ Fill the blanks with appropriate propositions

1. I picked _____ French when I study Economics in Paris University.
2. After returning from the countryside, he devoted his spare time _____ gardening.
3. She eats so little because she is going _____ a diet.

4. A big fire was put _____ yesterday night in the center of the city.

5. When dining in a restaurant, I prefer _____ sit near the window.

6. This area is covered _____ all kinds of trees.

7. To prevent him _____ spending too much time on playing games, his mother sold the computer.

8. Now please pay attention _____ the chairman's speech.

9. Do you approve _____ this proposal?

10. I agree _____ with Professor Li's idea.

Lesson 76

April Fools' Day
愚人节

I *Use the word(s) to make sentence(s)*

Possible

_____.

Possible — finish

_____.

Possible — finish — before Friday

_____.

Wander

_____.

Wander — get lost

_____.

Wander — get lost — forest

_____.

Survive

_____.

Survive — flood

_____.

Survive — flood — lucky

_____.

II Practice the key patterns

T: drive a car — three years

S1: How long have you driving a car?

S2: I have been driving a car for nearly three years.

Practice: (1) surf online — eight years

(2) study in college — two years

(3) work in Japan — four years

(4) live in this town — half a year

T: use chopsticks

S1: Have you been used to using chopsticks?

S2: Not yet. But soon I will get used to it.

Practice: (1) eat hot food

(2) bath in cold water

(3) work at night

(4) get up at five o'clock

T: ride your bicycle — repair

S1: Why don't you ride your bicycle?

S2: It is being repaired now.

Practice: (1) wear your green T — shirt — wash

(2) wear your watch — mend

(3) live in your apartment — decorate

III Retell the story

Firstly complete the blanks and remember what you said.

'To end our special news bulletin,' said the voice of the television announcer, 'we're going over to the macaroni fields of Calabria. Macaroni has been grown in this area for over six hundred years. Two of the _____, Giuseppe Moldova and

Riccardo Brabante, tell me that they have been _____

_____ this year and _____ . Here you can see

two workers who, between them, have just _____

_____ of golden brown macaroni stalks. The whole village has been

working day and night _____ this year's crop

before the September rains. On the right, you can see Mrs Brabante

herself. She has been helping her husband for thirty years now. Mrs

Brabante is talking to _____ where the crop is

processed. This last scene shows you what will happen at the end of

the harvest: the famous Calabrian macaroni-eating competition!

Signor Fratelli, the present champion, has _____ since

1991. And that ends our _____ for today, Thursday,

April 1st. We're now going back to the studio. '

Secondly retell the story in the third person.

Ⅳ Active questions

1. What is grown in this area?
2. How long is it been grown here?
3. Who are two of the leading growers?
4. What have they been expecting this year?
5. What has the whole village been doing day and night?
6. Who is Mrs. Brabante talking to?
7. What does the last scene show us?
8. What is the date today?

Lesson 77

A successful operation
一例成功的手术

> ### I   Use the word (s) to make sentence (s)

Illness

_____.

Illness — confine

_____.

Illness — confine — bed

_____.

Regret

_____.

Regret — tell

_____.

Regret — tell — secret

_____.

Heavy rain

_____.

Heavy rain — spoil

_____.

Heavy rain — spoil — garden

_____.

II Practice the key patterns

T: doctor

S1: What would you like to be in the future?

S2: I would like to be a doctor.

Practice: (1) dentist

(2) scientist

(3) lawyer

(4) engineer

T: they — come back — be back

S1: Did they come back last week?

S2: Yes. They have been back for a week.

Practice: (1) the film — start — be on

(2) she — come — be waiting

(3) he — go to work — be at work

(4) the family — go for trip — be away

T: do the laundry

S1: What are you going to do this weekend?

S2: I was told to do the laundry this weekend.

Practice: (1) work on the project

(2) pack up my belongings

(3) hand out the questionnaire

(4) analyze the data collected

III Retell the story

Firstly complete the blanks and remember what you said.

The mummy of an Egyptian woman who died in 800 B. C. has just _____. The mummy is that of Shepenmut who was once a singer in the Temple of Thebes. As there were _____

_____ on the X-ray plates taken of the mummy, doctors have been trying to find out whether the woman _____. The only way to do this was to operate. The operation, which _____ _____, proved to be very difficult because of _____ _____. The doctors removed a section of the mummy and _____. They also found something which the X-ray plates did not _____ of the god Duamutef. This god which has the head of a cow was normally placed inside a mummy. The doctors have not yet decided how the woman died. They feared that the mummy would _____ when they cut it open, but fortunately this has not happened. The mummy successfully _____.

Secondly retell the story in the third person.

Ⅳ Active questions

1. When did the mummy die?
2. What did the woman do when she was alive?
3. What have the doctors been trying to find out?
4. What was the only way to do?
5. How long did the operation last for?
6. Why was the operation very difficult?
7. What did they also find?
8. Where the god was usually placed?
9. What did the doctors fear?
10. Did the mummy survive the operation?

Lesson 78

The last one?

最后一支吗?

I *Use the word (s) to make sentence (s)*

Repeat

_____.

Repeat — question

_____.

Repeat — question — hear

_____.

Delighted

_____.

Delighted — news

_____.

Delighted — news — success

_____.

Urge

_____.

Urge — invest

_____.

Urge — invest — stocks

_____.

II Practice the key patterns

T: go shopping with you

S1: Would you mind my going shopping with you?

S2: Not at all.

Practice: (1) smoke in this room

(2) park here

(3) go to the exhibition with you

(4) buy the same coat with yours

T: write your thesis — three days

S1: Have you finished writing your thesis?

S2: Yes. I finished writing it three days ago.

Practice: (1) make a plan — two days

(2) do the experiment — two hours

(3) write the short story — a month

(4) go over the lessons — a week

T: meet Henry — next month

S1: When did you meet Henry last time?

S2: Last week. And I will meet him again next month.

Practice: (1) make a journey — this June

(2) read *China Daily* — next week

(3) give a presentation — next Friday

III Retell the story

Firstly complete the blanks and remember what you said.

After reading an article entitled 'Cigarette Smoking and Your Health', I lit a cigarette to _____ . I smoked _____

_____ as I was sure that this would be my last cigarette.

For a whole week I did not smoke at all and during this time, my

wife _____. I had all the usual symptoms of
someone giving up smoking: _____. My
friends kept on offering me cigarettes and cigars. They made no effort
to _____ whenever I _____
from my pocket. After seven days of this I went to a party.
Everybody around me was smoking and I felt _____
_____. When my old friend Brian _____, it was
more than I could bear. I took one guiltily, lit it and smoked with
satisfaction. My wife was delighted that things had _____
_____. Anyway, as Brian pointed out, it is the easiest thing in
the world to _____. He himself has done it lots of
times!

Secondly retell the story in the third person.

IV Active questions

1. What was the title of the article?
2. What was I sure as I smoked?
3. How long didn't I smoke at all?
4. What are the usual symptoms of someone giving up smoking?
5. What did my friends keep on doing?
6. Who urged me to accept a cigarette?
7. Why was my wife delighted?
8. What is the easiest in the world in Brian's viewpoint?

V Translate the following sentences into English

1. 他是个非常有名的政治家。
2. 作为同学，你们不该嘲笑他，而应该帮助他。
3. 要是这台电脑有问题，请给我打电话。
4. 除非他好好复习，要不然这次考试会不及格。

5. 他总是给他的学生很多鼓励，让他们充满自信。
6. 她头脑中慢慢产生了这样一个念头。
7. 这个暑假他们一家准备去海南旅游。
8. 这部电影不适合儿童看。
9. 她被雨淋了，感冒了。
10. 大学毕业后他进了一家外企。

Lesson 79 By air 乘飞机

I. Use the word(s) to make sentence(s).

Curious

_____ .

Curious — know

_____ .

Curious — know — intention

_____ .

Responsible

_____ .

Responsible — project

_____ .

Responsible — project — this semester

_____ .

Struggle

_____ .

Struggle — difficult

_____ .

Struggle — difficult — succeed

_____ .

II Practice the key patterns

T: California — the South America

S1: Where are you living now?

S2: Now I am living in California. I used to live in South America.

Practice: (1) New York — Chicago

(2) London — Beijing

(3) Hangzhou — Nanjing

(4) Philadelphia — Canada

T: talk to Nora over the phone

S1: What were you doing before I came in?

S2: I was talking to Nora over the phone.

Practice: (1) watch a horror movie

(2) read an interesting novel

(3) repair the radio

(4) iron my clothes

T: movie — boring

S1: What do you think of the movie?

S2: This is the most boring movie I have ever seen.

Practice: (1) performance — excellent

(2) show — splendid

(3) exhibition — gorgeous

(4) graduation ceremony — exciting

III Retell the story

Firstly complete the blanks and remember what you said.

I used to _____ when I was a boy. My parents used to live in South America and I used to fly there from Europe in the holidays. A flight attendant would _____

_____ and I never had an unpleasant experience. I am used to traveling by air and only on one occasion have I ever _____

_____. After taking off, we were flying low over the city and slowly _____, when the plane _____ and flew back to the airport. While we were waiting to land, a flight attendant told us to _____ as soon as it had touched down. Everybody on board was worried and we were _____. Later we learnt that there was a very important person on board. The police had been told that _____. After we had landed, the plane was _____. Fortunately, nothing was found and five hours later we were able to take off again.

Secondly retell the story in the third person.

Ⅳ Active questions

1. What did I use to do when I was a boy?
2. Where did my parents use to live?
3. Who would take charge of me?
4. What happened after the plane took off?
5. What did a flight attendant tell us to do?
6. What did we learn later?
7. Was anything found on the plane?
8. When were we able to take off again?

Lesson 80

The Crystal Palace

水晶宫

I Use the word(s) to make sentence(s)

Persistent

_____.

Persistent — accept

_____.

Persistent — accept — criticism

_____.

Collect

_____.

Collect — information

_____.

Collect — information — topic

_____.

Expect

_____.

Expect — arrive

_____.

Expect — arrive — in time

_____.

II Practice the key patterns

T: move into your new apartment — decorate

S1: Have you moved into your new apartment?

S2: Not yet. It is being decorated now.

Practice: (1) hand in your report — write

(2) make out a sketch plan — draft

(3) pass the oral defense of the graduation thesis — prepare

T: exhausted — work the whole day

S1: What have you been doing? You look exhausted.

S2: I have been working the whole day.

Practice: (1) thirsty — run for two hours

(2) hungry — climb the whole day

(3) angry — quarrel with my sister the whole morning

(4) upset — worry about my dad's heart disease

T: attend the conference — be free

S1: Will you attend the conference tomorrow?

S2: I will attend it if I am free.

Practice: (1) climb the Xiangshan Mountain — it is sunny

(2) join the activity — it is interesting

(3) go to the party — not have to work overtime

III Retell the story

Firstly complete the blanks and remember what you said.

Perhaps the _____ of the nineteenth century was the Crystal Palace, which was built in _____ for the Great Exhibition of 1851. The Crystal Palace was _____, for it was made of iron and glass. It was one of the biggest buildings of all time and a lot of people from many countries

came to see it. A great many goods were _____
from various parts of the world. There was also _____
_____. The most wonderful piece of machinery on show was
Nasmyth's steam hammer. Though in those days, traveling was not
as easy as it is today, steam boats carried _____
across the Channel from Europe. On arriving in England, they were
taken to the Crystal Palace by train. There were six million visitors in
all, and the profits from the exhibition were used to _____
_____. Later, the Crystal Palace was moved to South London. It
remained one of the most famous buildings in the world until it was

_____.

Secondly retell the story in the third person.

Ⅳ Active questions

1. Where was the Crystal Palace built?
2. Why was it different from all other building in the world?
3. What were sent to the exhibition?
4. What were also on display?
5. What was the most wonderful piece of machinery on show?
6. How were the visitors carried to the palace?
7. How many visitors were there in all?
8. What were the profits used to do?
9. Where was the Crystal Palace moved to?
10. When was the palace burnt down?

Lesson 81

Escape

逃脱

I Use the word(s) to make sentence(s)

Intend

_____.

Intend — deal

_____.

Intend — deal — incident

_____.

Show

_____.

Show — operate

_____.

Show — operate — machine

_____.

Inform

_____.

Inform — notice

_____.

Inform — notice — meeting

II Practice the key patterns

T: make a trip to Qingdao

S1: What did you do this May Day Holiday?

S2: I made a trip to Qingdao this May Day Holiday.

Practice: (1) visit my grandparents in the countryside

(2) visit the World Park

(3) go to Jay Zhou's concert

T: miss the train — stay up late

S1: Why did you miss the train yesterday?

S2: Because I stayed up late the day before yesterday.

Practice: (1) fall asleep during the meeting — be too tired

(2) lose the job — be too lazy

(3) be scolded by the teacher — fail the exam

(4) break your leg — have an accident

T: return the book

S1: Have you returned the book?

S2: Not yet. I will return it soon.

Practice: (1) conduct the survey

(2) hand out the teaching materials

(3) fix the window

(4) buy the copying machine

III Retell the story

Firstly complete the blanks and remember what you said.

When he had _____, the prisoner of war quickly dragged him into the bushes. Working rapidly in the darkness, he soon _____. Now, dressed in a blue uniform and with _____, the prisoner _____

_____ up and down in front of the camp. He could hear shouting in the camp itself. Lights were blazing and men were running here and there: they had just discovered that _____

_____ . At that moment, a large black car with four officers inside it, stopped at the camp gates. The officers got out and the prisoner _____ . When they had gone, the driver of the car came towards him. The man obviously wanted to talk. He was rather elderly with grey hair and clear blue eyes. The prisoner _____ , but there was nothing else he could do. As the man came near, the prisoner _____ .

Then, jumping into the car, he drove off as quickly as he could.

Secondly retell the story in the third person.

IV **Active questions**

1. Who was quickly dragged into the bushes?
2. What did the prisoner of war do in the darkness?
3. Now what was he dressed in?
4. What was over his shoulder?
5. What could he hear in the camp?
6. What had they discovered?
7. Who was in the large black car?
8. What did he do when the officers got out?
9. What did the driver of the car look like?
10. What did the prisoner do as the driver came near?

V **Fill the blanks with the correct form of the verbs given**

1. The little boy dreamed of _____ a scientist. (become)
2. I have not _____ to him since I left China. (call)
3. This radio needs _____ . (repair)

4. _____ it or not, he has written four papers this semester. (believe)

5. He has _____ English for ten years. (teach)

6. She is an expert at _____. (draw)

7. I prefer _____ in China rather than abroad. (live)

8. He was _____ about the accident when the rain started. (inquire)

9. They had trouble _____ out the experiment. (carry)

10. Do you mind _____ away the rubbish for me? (throw)

Lesson
82

Monster or fish?
是妖还是鱼？

I Use the word (s) to make sentence (s)

Instruct

_____.

Instruct — teacher

_____.

Instruct — teacher — understand

_____.

Manage

_____.

Manage — rescue

_____.

Manage — rescue — flood

_____.

Suppose

_____.

Suppose — lose

_____.

Suppose — lose — stop

_____.

Ⅱ Practice the key patterns

T: cook the supper

S1: Will you cook the supper today?

S2: Yes. I have cooked it.

Practice: (1) clean the floor

　　　　(2) iron the clothes

　　　　(3) buy the beautiful dress

　　　　(4) send a Christmas card to your uncle

T: water the garden — at once

S1: You should have watered the garden now.

S2: Sorry. I will water the garden at once.

Practice: (1) hand in your homework — soon

　　　　(2) wash the clothes — immediately

　　　　(3) make a phone call to my aunt — in a minute

　　　　(4) rewrite your essay — on the instant

T: work for a long time — five years

S1: Has she been working for a long time?

S2: Yes. She has been working for five years.

Practice: (1) study in college for a long time — four years

　　　　(2) live in this place for a short time — half a year

　　　　(3) be in love with Tom for a long time — three years

Ⅲ Retell the story

Firstly complete the blanks and remember what you said.

Fishermen and sailors sometimes claim to ＿＿＿＿＿

＿＿＿. Though people have often ＿＿＿＿＿＿＿＿＿, it

is now known that many of these 'monsters' which have at times

been sighted are ＿＿＿＿＿＿＿＿. Occasionally,

_____, but they are rarely caught out at sea. Some time ago, however, _____ near Madagascar. A small fishing boat was carried miles out to sea by the powerful fish as it _____. Realizing that this was no ordinary fish, the fisherman _____ in any way. When it was eventually brought to shore, it was found to be _____. It had a head like a horse, big blue eyes, shining silver skin, and _____. The fish, which has since been sent to a museum where it is _____ _____, is called an oarfish. Such creatures have rarely been seen alive by man as they live at a depth of six hundred feet.

Secondly retell the story in the third person.

Ⅳ Active questions

1. What do fishermen and sailors sometimes claim to do?
2. What have people often laughed at?
3. In fact, what are the "monsters" that have been sighted?
4. Where a peculiar fish was caught some time ago?
5. How did the fish pull the fishing boat?
6. What did the fisherman realize?
7. What did the peculiar look like?
8. Where has the fish been sent?

After the elections

大选之后

I *Use the word (s) to make sentence (s)*

March

_____.

March — demand

_____.

March — demand — better

_____.

Defeat

_____.

Defeat — competition

_____.

Defeat — competition — sad

_____.

Suspicious

_____.

Suspicious — behavior

_____.

Suspicious — behavior — attention

_____.

II　Practice the key patterns

T:　miss the bus ← take a cab

S1: What would you do if you missed the bus?

S2: If I missed the bus, I would take a cab.

Practice: (1) lose the way — refer to the map

(2) be in Japan — visit Tokyo

(3) be on a holiday — go to the entertainment park

(4) get sick — ask for a day off

T:　happy — smile the whole day

S1: It sees that Lily was very happy.

S2: Yes. She was so happy that she smiled the whole day.

Practice: (1) angry — lose her temper

(2) worried — cannot fall asleep the whole night

(3) nervous — keep stammering

T:　leave for Hong Kong this Thursday

S1: What are you going to do?

S2: I am leaving for Hong Kong this Thursday.

Practice: (1) read a novel in the study

(2) go to visit my headmaster

(3) visit the Military Museum

(4) go to a concert this Wednesday

III　Retell the story

Firstly complete the blanks and remember what you said.

The former Prime Minister, Mr. Wentworth Lane, was _____

_____. He is now _____ and

has gone abroad. My friend, Patrick, has always been _____

_____ of Mr. Lane's Radical Progressive Party. After the

elections, Patrick went to the former Prime Minister's house. When he asked if Mr. Lane lived there, _____ told him that since his defeat, the ex-Prime Minister had gone abroad. On the following day, Patrick went to the house again. The same policeman was just _____, when Patrick asked the same question. Though _____, the policeman gave him the same answer. The day after, Patrick went to the house once more and asked exactly the same question. This time, the policeman ____

_____. 'I told you yesterday and the day before yesterday,' he shouted, 'Mr. Lane was defeated in the elections. He has retired from political life and gone to live abroad!' 'I know,' answered Patrick, 'but I _____!'

Secondly retell the story in the third person.

IV Active questions

1. Who was defeated in the recent elections?
2. What is he doing now?
3. Who was Patrick?
4. What did Patrick do after the elections?
5. What did the policeman answer to Patrick's question the first time?
6. What did Patrick do the following day?
7. What did the policeman feel the third day?
8. Why did Patrick keep asking the same question?

Lesson
84

On strike

罢工

I Use the word(s) to make sentence(s)

Object

_____ .

Object — plan

_____ .

Object — plan — inappropriate

_____ .

Disguise

_____ .

Disguise — interest

_____ .

Disguise — interest — laughter

_____ .

Accustom

_____ .

Accustom — weather

_____ .

Accustom — weather — country

_____ .

II Practice the key patterns

T: in the gym — exercise

S1: Is Bill in the gym?

S2: Yes. He has been exercising all morning.

Practice: (1) in the study — study

(2) in the park — play games with kids

(3) in the sitting room — play chess with his friends

(4) in the hospital — look after the sick grandpa

T: in the shopping mall — study

S1: I saw you in the shopping mall yesterday afternoon.

S2: You must have made a mistake. I was studying yesterday afternoon.

Practice: (1) in the cinema — work

(2) in the market — draw a picture

(3) in the office — be on a holiday

(4) in the gym — watch a movie

T: go to the tea party — type the paper

S1: When will you go to the tea party?

S2: I will go to the tea party after I type the paper.

Practice: (1) go to the theatre — have a shower

(2) go to the hospital — have breakfast

(3) go to the railway station — pack my belongings

(4) go to the Smith's — finish my homework

III Retell the story

Firstly complete the blanks and remember what you said.

Busmen have decided to ＿＿＿＿＿＿＿ next week. The strike is due to begin on Tuesday. No one knows ＿＿＿＿＿＿＿

_____. The busmen have stated that the strike will _____ _____ about pay and working conditions. Most people believe that the strike will _____. Many owners of private cars are going to offer '_____' to people on their way to work. This will _____ to some extent. Meanwhile, a number of university students have _____ _____ while the strike lasts. All the students are expert drivers, but before they drive any of the buses, they will have to _____. The students are going to take the test in two days' time. Even so, people are going to find it difficult to get to work. But so far, the public has _____ in letters to the Press. Only one or two people have objected that the students will drive too fast!

Secondly retell the story in the third person.

Ⅳ Active questions

1. What have busmen decide to do?
2. When is this strike due to begin?
3. What have the busmen stated?
4. What do most people believe?
5. What are many owners of private cars going to do?
6. What have a number of university students volunteer to do?
7. What will the students have to do before they drive buses?
8. Why only one or two people have objected?

Ⅴ Translate the following sentences into English

1. 我猜不出他们什么时候回来。
2. 他在公交车上丢了钱包。
3. 真不好意思，我被交通堵塞耽误了。

4. 我不喜欢他说话的语气。

5. 他 20 年来一直住在这个城市里。

6. 她很后悔，把自己关在屋子里一天不出来。

7. 即使请医生，她的病也治不好了。

8. 她 12 岁进了国家游泳队。

9. 昨天这个时候我正在看足球。

10. 他准备高考后去国外念大学。

I Use the word (s) to make sentence (s)

Evade

_____.

Evade — responsibility

_____.

Evade — responsibility — leave

_____.

Evil

_____.

Evil — intention

_____.

Evil — intention — corrupt

_____.

Shock

_____.

Shock — news

_____.

Shock — news — get married

_____.

II Practice the key patterns

T: have dinner

S1: Are they having dinner now?

S2: I suppose they have finished dinner now.

Practice: (1) have a rest

(2) walk the dog

(3) do the shopping

(4) have a discussion

T: visit Tom — be at home

S1: Shall we visit Tom today?

S2: Yes. He will be at home the whole day.

Practice: (1) have a talk with Lisa — practice piano

(2) discuss with Henry — revise the paper

(3) talk to Allen over the phone — clean the house

T: stay at the college — another week

S1: How much longer will you be staying at the college?

S2: I will be staying at the college for another week.

Practice: (1) stay at the hotel — three days

(2) stay at his uncle's house — a month

(3) study abroad — two years

(4) work in New York — half a year

III Retell the story

Firstly complete the blanks and remember what you said.

I have just _____ from my old school, informing me that my former headmaster, Mr. Stuart Page, will ____ _____. Pupils of the school, old and new, will be _____ _____. All those who have contributed towards the gift will _____ which will be sent to the headmaster's home. We shall all remember Mr. Page for his _____

_____ he gave us when we went so unwillingly to school. A great many former pupils will be _____ next Thursday. It is _____ that the day before his retirement, Mr. Page will have been teaching for a total of forty years. After he has retired, he will _____. For him, this will be _____. But this does not matter, for, as he has often remarked, one is never too old to learn.

Secondly retell the story in the third person.

Ⅳ *Active questions*

1. What does the letter inform me?
2. Who will be retiring next week?
3. What will the pupils of the school do?
4. Which kind of present will be sent to the headmaster's home?
5. What shall we remember Mr. Page for?
6. What is the curious coincidence?
7. What will he do after retirement?
8. What has he often remarked?

Lesson 86

Out of control

失控

I Use the word(s) to make sentence(s)

Retire

_____.

Retire — devote

_____.

Retire — devote — chess

_____.

Train

_____.

Train — for years

_____.

Train — for years — succeed

_____.

Acquire

_____.

Acquire — knowledge

_____.

Acquire — knowledge — university

_____.

II Practice the key patterns

T: get up early — catch the early train

S1: Why did you get up so early?

S2: Because I wanted to catch the early train.

Practice: (1) have supper so hurriedly — see the movie at six o'clock

(2) stay up so late — finish my composition

(3) come to school so early — talk to Mr. Li about the thesis

T: fail his chemistry exam — not study hard

S1: Jack failed his chemistry exam.

S2: That's not surprising. He did not study hard.

Practice: (1) miss the bus — not get up early

(2) break his leg — be not careful

(3) be defeated in the contest — prepare well

(4) be fired — not work hard enough

T: white coat — red one

S1: Do you like this white coat?

S2: Well. I prefer the red one.

Practice: (1) blue T-shirt — pink one

(2) yellow blouse — purple one

(3) round table — square one

(4) red vase — green one

III Retell the story

Firstly complete the blanks and remember what you said.

As the man tried to _____, the steering wheel came away in his hands. He _____, who had been water skiing for the last fifteen minutes. Both men had hardly had time to realize what was happening when they were _____ . The speedboat had struck a buoy, but it continued to __ _____ . Both men had just begun to swim towards the shore, when they noticed with dismay that the speedboat was _____ . It now came straight towards them at tremendous speed. In less than a minute, it _____ only a few feet away. After it had passed, they swam on as quickly as they could because they knew that the boat would soon return. They had just _____ when the boat again _____ _____ . On this occasion, however, it had slowed down considerably. The petrol had nearly all been _____ . Before long, the noise dropped completely and the boat began to _____ _____ .

Secondly retell the story in the third person.

Ⅳ *Active questions*

1. What did the man try to do?
2. What had his companion been doing?
3. What had the men hardly had time to realize?
4. What did the men notice when they began to swim towards the shore?
5. How fast was the speedboat moving?
6. Why did the men swim as quickly as they could?
7. What had nearly all been used up?
8. When did the noise drop completely?

Lesson 87

A perfect alibi
极好的不在犯罪现场的证据

I Use the word (s) to make sentence (s)

Catch

_____.

Catch — attention

_____.

Catch — attention — guard

_____.

Gather

_____.

Gather — gate

_____.

Gather — gate — quarrel

_____.

Remind

_____.

Remind — college days

_____.

Remind — college days — happy

_____.

II Practice the key patterns

T: eat ice cream — go on a diet

S1: Why didn't Mary eat ice cream?

S2: Because the doctor suggested her that she should go on a diet.

Practice: (1) do morning exercise — lose some weight

(2) quit his present job — join a trading cooperation

(3) study harder — enter a good university

T: know the result — come out by the end of May

S1: When will you know the result?

S2: The result will have come out by the end of May.

Practice: (1) finish the paper — be completed by next Wednesday

(2) hand in your report — be handed in by June

(3) water the flowers — be watered by this afternoon

(4) sweep the floor — be swept by 5 o'clock

T: go fishing — go shopping

S1: Would you like to go fishing?

S2: I'd prefer to go shopping.

Practice: (1) go for a walk — go swimming

(2) buy the red wallet — buy the white one

(3) have a trip — have a picnic

(4) visit the Art Museum — visit the Imperial Palace

III Retell the story

Firstly complete the blanks and remember what you said.

'At the time _____, I was traveling on the 8 o'clock train to London,' said the man.

'Do you always _____?' asked the inspector.

'Of course I do,' answered the man. 'I must be at work at 10 o'clock. My employer will confirm that I was there on time.'

'Would _____?' asked the inspector.

'I suppose it would, but I never catch a later train.'

'At what time did you arrive at the station?'

'At ten to eight. I _____.'

'And you didn't _____?'

'Of course not.'

'I suggest,' said the inspector, 'that you are not _____

_____. I suggest that you did not catch the 8 o'clock train, but that you caught the 8:25 which would still get you to work on time. You see, on the morning of the murder, the 8 o'clock train did not run at all. It _____.'

Secondly retell the story in the third person.

Ⅳ Active questions

1. What was the man doing when the murder was committed?

2. Does he always catch such an early train?

3. What will the man's employer confirm?

4. Would a later train get the man to work on time?

5. What did the man do at the station?

6. Did he notice anything unusual?

7. Which train did the suspect take actually?

8. How did the inspector know that he was telling a lie?

Ⅴ Fill the blanks with appropriate propositions

1. Please talk to Mr. Bin because he is in charge _____ this project.

2. She went to the airport to see her boyfriend _____

3. They visit their parents _____ times.

4. It is said that this castle is haunted _____ a ghost.

5. He didn't wake _____ until ten o'clock this morning.

6. All the boys in this class are fond _____ playing basketball.

7. She gazed _____ the theatre for a while.

8. His car broke _____ on his way to the office.

9. She has been searching _____ her watch in her room the whole day.

10. Kate is standing _____ the window, with a coffee cup in her hand.

Lesson 88

Trapped in a mine

困在矿井里

I Use the word(s) to make sentence(s)

Wonder

_____ .

Wonder — real intention

_____ .

Wonder — real intention — join the activity

_____ .

Suggest

_____ .

Suggest — accept

_____ .

Suggest — accept — job

_____ .

Earthquake

_____ .

Earthquake — harm

_____ .

Earthquake — harm — human beings

_____ .

II Practice the key patterns

T: the machine — function well

S1: What do you know about the machine?

S2: It is said to be functioning well.

Practice: (1) the new officer — work very efficiently

(2) the refrigerator — cool the food very quickly

(3) the juice extractor — work well

T: read while sitting on a bus

S1: Look, she is reading.

S2: She'd better not read while sitting on a bus.

Practice: (1) sing while having a sore throat

(2) read in the sun

(3) type while the finger is hurt

(4) walk while the ankle is hurt

T: be late for work — come earlier

S1: You should not have been late for work.

S2: Sorry. I will come earlier next time.

Practice: (1) miss the bus — catch it

(2) hurt her feelings — be kind to her

(3) hurt your ankle — protect myself

(4) distract in the conference — be attentive

III Retell the story

Firstly complete the blanks and remember what you said.

Six men have been _____ for seventeen hours. If they are not brought to the surface soon they may _____ _____. However, rescue operations are _____. If explosives are used, vibrations will cause the roof of the mine to

collapse. Rescue workers are therefore _____
of the mine. They intend to _____. If there
had not been a hard layer of rock beneath the soil, they would have
completed the job in a few hours. As it is, they have been drilling for
sixteen hours and they still have a long way to go. Meanwhile, a
microphone, which was _____ two hours ago, has
enabled the men to _____. Though they are
running out of food and drink, the men are _____
that they will get out soon. They have been told that _____
_____. If they knew how difficult it was to drill through the hard
rock, they would _____.

Secondly retell the story in the third person.

Ⅳ Active questions

1. How long have six men been trapped in a mine?
2. What may happen if they are not brought to the surface soon?
3. What will happen if explosives are used?
4. What are rescue workers doing?
5. What do they intend to do?
6. How long have they been drilling?
7. What has the microphone enabled the men trapped to do?
8. What have the men in a mine been told?

A slip of the tongue

口误

I Use the word (s) to make sentence (s)

Complain

_____ .

Complain — price

_____ .

Complain — price — low wages

_____ .

Holiday

_____ .

Holiday — spoil

_____ .

Holiday — spoil — heavy rain

_____ .

Bear

_____ .

Bear — rude behavior

_____ .

Bear — rude behavior — at the party

_____ .

II Practice the key patterns

T: not answer the call — in the dean's office

S1: I gave you a call this morning but you did not answer it.

S2: I must have been in the dean's office.

Practice: (1) not answer the door — in a shower

(2) not at home — buy food in the market

(3) not respond to my shouting — attentively do my homework

T: involve in an accident

S1: I have been waiting for you for three hours.

S2: Sorry. I was involved in an accident.

Practice: (1) delay by a phone call from the office

(2) require to finish the project plan

(3) not allow to leave before ten o'clock

T: Jim called you — read a magazine

S1: What were you doing when Jim called you?

S2: I was reading a vogue magazine.

Practice: (1) Lucy rushed in — mend the electric fan

(2) Tom broke the glass — cook in the kitchen

(3) it started to rain — on the way home

(4) Julia knocked the door — practice piano

III Retell the story

Firstly complete the blanks and remember what you said.

People will do anything to _____ — even if it is a bad one. When the news got round that _____ _____ by the P. and U. Bird Seed Company, we all rushed to see it. We had to _____ and there must have been several hundred people present just before the show began. Unfortunately, the show was _____. Those who failed to get in need not have _____, as many of the artistes who should have appeared did not come. The only funny things we heard that evening came from _____. He was _____ and for some minutes stood awkwardly before the microphone. As soon as he opened his mouth, everyone _____. We all know what the poor man should have said, but what he actually said was: 'This is the Poo and Ee Seed Bird Company. Good ladies, evening and gentlemen!'

Secondly retell the story in the third person.

Ⅳ Active questions

1. What will people do anything for?
2. What was the news?
3. What did we have to do to get in?
4. Was the show interesting?
5. When did the funny thing happen?
6. Was the advertiser nervous?
7. What did everyone do as soon as he opened his mouth?
8. What did the advertiser actually said?
9. What should he have said?

Lesson 90

What's for supper?
晚餐吃什么？

I Use the word (s) to make sentence (s)

Proud

_____.

Proud — serve

_____.

Proud — serve — our country

_____.

Terrify

_____.

Terrify — horrible

_____.

Terrify — horrible — cry

_____.

Painting

_____.

Painting — express

_____.

Painting — express — attitude

_____.

II Practice the key patterns

T: fail the exam — better prepare the exam

S1: I failed the math exam.

S2: If I were you, I would have better prepared the exam.

Practice: (1) break my leg — be more careful

(2) have an accident — drive more carefully

(3) be late for school — get up earlier

(4) get fired — work harder

T: pass the exam — take a trip to Hangzhou

S1: What will you do if you pass the exam?

S2: I will take a trip to Hangzhou.

Practice: (1) succeed in this project — have a party at home

(2) receive the invitation — go to attend the ceremony

(3) come across her at street — say hello to her

T: visit the Art Museum with my dad

S1: What are you going to do this weekend?

S2: I am going to visit the Art Museum with my dad.

Practice: (1) help grandpa to harvest crops

(2) eat barbeque in a restaurant

(3) attend a swimming competition

(4) go to my classmate's house

III Retell the story

Firstly complete the blanks and remember what you said.

Fish and chips has always been _____ in Britain, but as the oceans have been over-fished, fish has become more and more expensive. So it comes as a surprise to learn that _____ _____ on North Sea oil rigs. Oil rigs have to be _____

_____ and divers, who often have to work in darkness a hundred feet under water, have been _____ by giant fish bumping into them as they work. Now they have had special cages made to _____. The fish are not sharks or killer whales, but favorite eating varieties like cod and skate which _____, sometimes as much as twelve feet in length. Three factors have caused these fish to grow so large: _____ _____ round the hot oil pipes under the sea; the plentiful supply of food _____; _____ _____ around the oil rigs. As a result, the fish just eat and eat and grow and grow in the lovely warm water. Who eats who?

Secondly retell the story in the third person.

Ⅳ Active questions

1. What has always been a favorite dish in Britain?
2. Why does fish have become more and more expensive?
3. What are terrifying the divers on North Sea oil rig?
4. How deep do divers have to work?
5. What are made to protect the divers?
6. What are the fish?
7. How many factors have caused the fish to grow so large?
8. What are the factors respectively?

Ⅴ Translate the following sentences into English

1. 开始打雷的时候她正在操场上。
2. 去海南旅游期间他摔断了腿。
3. 他为在地震中遇难的人感到深深悲痛。
4. 她为自己是奥运志愿者而感到骄傲。
5. 自从去年分别后他们再也没见过面。

6. 这是十五年后他第一次回故乡。
7. 他们居然是兄妹，他感到十分震惊。
8. 据说这个周末电影院有好莱坞新片上映。
9. 她陷入了深深的不安和自责。
10. 他的前妻在一起交通事故中丧生。

Three men in a basket
三人同籃

I Use the word (s) to make sentence (s)

Terrify

_____ .

Terrify — cry

_____ .

Terrify — cry — at night

_____ .

Favorite

_____ .

Favorite — hobby

_____ .

Favorite — hobby — model trains

_____ .

Arrest

_____ .

Arrest — murder

_____ .

Arrest — murder — regret

_____ .

II Practice the key patterns

T: tell — write the thesis

S1: What did you do yesterday?

S2: I was told to write the thesis yesterday.

Practice: (1) order — look after the little sister

(2) command — clean the dining room

(3) inform — hand in the summary

T: happy — summer holiday is coming

S1: You look happy.

S2: Yes. I am happy because the summer holiday is coming.

Practice: (1) worried — final exams are coming

(2) disappointed — Peter was defeated in the contest

(3) sad — fail the English mid — exam

(4) jealous — Lily did better in the exam than me

T: post the parcel

S1: Have you posted the parcel?

S2: Not yet. I am going to post it this afternoon.

Practice: (1) mend the fridge

(2) put away the clothes

(3) clear the room

(4) feed the cat

III Retell the story

Firstly complete the blanks and remember what you said.

A pilot _____ which seemed to be making for a Royal Air Force Station nearby. He informed the station at once, but no one there was _____. The officer in the control tower was very angry when he heard the news, because balloons can be _____. He said that someone might be _____ and the pilot was ordered to _____ _____. The pilot managed to circle the balloon for some time. He could make out three men in a basket under it and one of them was _____. When the balloon was over the station, the pilot saw one of the men taking photographs. Soon afterwards, the balloon began to _____. The police were called in, but they could not arrest anyone, for the basket contained two Members of Parliament and the Commanding Officer of the station! As the Commanding Officer explained later, one half of the station did not know _____!

Secondly retell the story in the third person.

IV *Active questions* ....

1. What did the pilot notice?

2. Who was very angry when he heard the news?

3. Why was he very angry?

4. What was the pilot ordered to do?

5. How many people were there in the basket?

6. What did the pilot see when the balloon was over the station?

7. Why couldn't the police arrest anyone?

8. What did the Commanding Officer explain later?

Lesson 92

Asking for trouble
自找麻烦

I Use the word(s) to make sentence(s)

Nervous

_____.

Nervous — exam

_____.

Nervous — exam — fail

_____.

Confident

_____.

Confident — pass

_____.

Confident — pass — test

_____.

Lucky

_____.

Lucky — escape

_____.

Lucky — escape — collapse

_____.

II Practice the key patterns

T: work here — one year

S1: How long have you been working here?

S2: I have been working here for one year. But I still haven't got
     used to working here.

Practice: (1) live here — half a year

           (2) wear glasses — three months

           (3) wear makeup — one month

T: clean the room

S1: You should have cleaned the room.

S2: Sorry. I will clean it right now.

Practice: (1) boil the water

           (2) cook the meal

           (3) iron the clothes

           (4) wash the car

T: attend the party — not have to do the experiment

S1: Do you know if Jim will attend the party?

S2: He told me that he would come if he did not have to do the
experiment.

Practice: (1) join the contest — have a good score

           (2) attend the meeting — be free

           (3) go hiking — be in a good humor

           (4) go to the concert — finish the homework

III Retell the story

Firstly complete the blanks and remember what you said.

It must have been about two in the morning when I returned
home. I tried to _____, but she was fast

asleep, so I _____, put it against the wall, and began climbing towards the bedroom window. I was almost there when a sarcastic voice below said, 'I don't think the windows _____ at this time of the night.' I looked down and nearly _____. I immediately _____ _____, but I said, 'I enjoy cleaning windows at night.' 'So do I,' answered the policeman in the same tone. 'Excuse my interrupting you. I hate to _____, but would you mind coming with me to the station?'

'Well, I'd prefer to stay here,' I said. 'You see, I've _____ _____.'

'Your what?' he called. 'My key,' I shouted.

Fortunately, the shouting woke up my wife who opened the window just as the policeman had _____.

Secondly retell the story in the third person.

Ⅳ Active questions

1. What was the time when I returned home?
2. What did I try to do?
3. Where did I get the ladder?
4. What did the sarcastic voice below say?
5. What did I answer to the voice?
6. What did the policeman answer in the same tone?
7. What woke up my wife?
8. Who opened the window?

Lesson 93

A noble gift

崇高的礼物

I Use the word (s) to make sentence (s) ....

Able

_____ .

Able — reach

_____ .

Able — reach — station

_____ .

Admire

_____ .

Admire — ability

_____ .

Admire — ability —

_____ .

Suggest

_____ .

Suggest — take a rest

_____ .

Suggest — take a rest — holiday

_____ .

Ⅱ Practice the key patterns

T: graduate from the college — enter a trading company

S1: What did you do after you graduated from the college?

S2: After I graduated from the college, I entered a trading company.

Practice: (1) lay the table — help to cook the meal

(2) get a master's degree in Harvard — start to purchase a doctor's degree

(3) leave the food company — set up a company of his own

(4) do the washing — go shopping with my best friend

T: Jon — in the office — in the classroom

S1: I saw Jon in the office.

S2: You must have made a mistake. He is supposed to be in the classroom.

Practice: (1) Mary — in the street — write the composition in the study

(2) Carl — in the park — do the experiment in the lab

(3) Steve — at the party — attend the conference

T: meet Lisa — last December

S1: Did you meet Lisa recently?

S2: I have not met her since last December.

Practice: (1) write to Sam — last month

(2) call Susan — last weekend

(3) talk to Tim — the day before yesterday

(4) watch movie with Laura — last March

Ⅲ Retell the story

Firstly complete the blanks and remember what you said.

One of the _____ in the world, the Statue of

Liberty, was presented to the United States of America in the nineteenth century by the people of France. The great statue, which was _____, took ten years to complete. The actual figure was made of _____ which had been especially constructed by Eiffel. Before it could be _____ _____, a site had to be found for it and _____. The site chosen was an island at the entrance of New York Harbor. By 1884, a statue which was 151 feet tall had been erected in Paris. The following year, it was _____. By the end of October 1886, the statue had been _____ and it was officially presented to the American people by Bartholdi. Ever since then, the great monument has been _____ for the millions of people who have passed through New York Harbor to _____.

Secondly retell the story in the third person.

IV Active questions

1. What is one of the most famous monuments in the world?
2. When was it presented to the U. S. A. ?
3. Who presented it to the U. S. A. ?
4. Who designed the monument?
5. What was the monument made of?
6. What had to be done before it could be transported to the U. S. A. ?
7. When was the statue put together again?
8. For whom the monument has been a symbol of liberty?

V Fill the blanks with the correct form of the verbs given

1. The food is _____ away by her mother. (throw)

2. It is a _____ news and everyone was sad after hearing it. (disappoint)

3. She has been _____ to the dry weather in Beijing. (accustom)

4. He was very happy at her _____ at the party. (present)

5. Can you measure the _____ of the boat? (long)

6. This is such a _____ scene that she was scared to cry. (fright)

7. She was so _____ that I was taken in. (persuade)

8. He took to _____ after the death of his daughter in the earthquake. (drink)

9. I was _____ by the horrible accident. (frighten)

10. My father received the school report card with _____. (satisfy)

Lesson 94

Future champions

未来的冠军

I Use the word(s) to make sentence(s)

Obey

_____

Obey — rules

_____

Obey — rules — smoking

_____

Gaze

_____

Gaze — ask

_____

Gaze — ask — impatiently

_____

Supply

_____

Supply — poor people

_____

Supply — poor people — shelter

_____

II Practice the key patterns

T: decline your invitation

S1: What would you do if she declines your invitation?

S2: I have no idea. What do you think I should do?

Practice: (1) hurt your feeling

(2) break her leg

(3) fall in love with your classmate

(4) get fired

T: go to Hainan alone — be independent

S1: Why did you go to Hainan alone?

S2: In order to be independent.

Practice: (1) apply for that job — earn more money

(2) study so hard — get a satisfactory score in the exam

(3) go abroad — learn more knowledge in this field

T: purchase a master's degree

S1: What do you in tend to do after graduation?

S2: I'd like to purchase a master's degree.

Practice: (1) join a transnational cooperation

(2) be a middle school English teacher

(3) a finance assistant

(4) a government official

III Retell the story

Firstly complete the blanks and remember what you said.

Experiments have proved that children can be _____

_____ at a very early age. At _____ in Los

Angeles, children become expert at _____ even

before they can walk. Babies of two months old do not appear to be

_____. It is not long before they are so _____

_____ that they can pick up weights from the floor of the

pool. A game that is very popular with these young swimmers is the

underwater tricycle race. Tricycles are _____ seven

feet under water. The children compete against each other to _____

_____. Many pedal their tricycles, but most of them

prefer to _____. Some children can _____

_____ without coming up for breath even once. Whether they will

ever become future Olympic champions, _____.

Meanwhile, they should encourage those among us who cannot swim

five yards before they are gasping for air.

Secondly retell the story in the third person.

Ⅳ Active questions

1. What do experiments have proved?
2. Where is the special swimming pool?
3. What are children expert at even before they can walk?
4. Do they soon become accustomed to swimming?
5. Which game is very popular with these young swimmers?
6. What are lined up on the floor of the pool?
7. What do children compete against each other to do?
8. What will time tell?

Lesson 95 A fantasy

纯属虚构

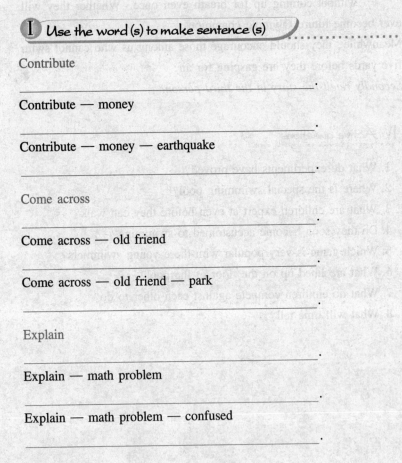

Ⅰ *Use the word (s) to make sentence (s)* ....

Contribute

_____.

Contribute — money

_____.

Contribute — money — earthquake

_____.

Come across

_____.

Come across — old friend

_____.

Come across — old friend — park

_____.

Explain

_____.

Explain — math problem

_____.

Explain — math problem — confused

_____.

II Practice the key patterns

T:　come to your house

S1:　Will Jack come to your house?

S2:　He said he will. But he hasn't appeared yet.

Practice:　(1) attend the party

(2) visit his uncle

(3) join the club activity

(4) eat barbeque with us

T:　paint the house — next week

S1:　When will the house be painted?

S2:　The house will have been painted next week.

Practice:　(1) repair the bicycle — next month

(2) complete the bridge — next June

(3) finish the paper — this Saturday

(4) build the road — next year

T:　get to the theatre — the play — start

S1:　What happened to you today?

S2:　When I got to the theatre, the play had started.

Practice:　(1) get to the airport — the plane — take off

(2) get to the ticket office — the tickets — sell out

(3) get to the railway station — the train — leave

III Retell the story

Firstly complete the blanks and remember what you said.

When the Ambassador of Escalopia returned home for lunch, his wife _____. He looked pale and his clothes were _____

_____.

'What has happened?' she asked. 'How did your clothes ____

_____?'

'A fire extinguisher, my dear,' answered the Ambassador dryly. 'University students set the Embassy on fire this morning.' 'Good heavens!' exclaimed his wife. 'And where were you at the time?' 'I was in my office as usual,' answered the Ambassador. 'The fire _____. I went down immediately, of course, and that fool, Horst, _____. He thought I was on fire. I must definitely _____.' The Ambassador's wife went on asking questions, when she suddenly __ _____. 'And how can you explain that?' she asked. 'Oh, that,' said the Ambassador. 'Someone _____ _____. Accurate, don't you think? Fortunately, I wasn't wearing it at the time. If I had been, I would not have been able to get home for lunch.'

Secondly retell the story in the third person.

Ⅳ **Active questions**

1. Who returned home for lunch?
2. Who got a shock?
3. What did she ask her husband?
4. What did the Ambassador answer dryly?
5. What did his wife exclaim?
6. Where did the fire break out?
7. What did Horst do to the Ambassador?
8. How did the Ambassador explain the big hole in his hat?

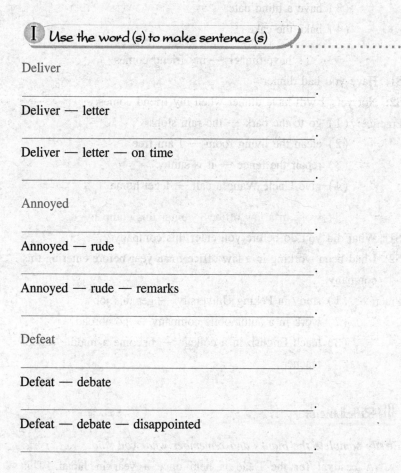

Lesson 96

The dead return

亡灵返乡

I Use the word(s) to make sentence(s)

Deliver

_____.

Deliver — letter

_____.

Deliver — letter — on time

_____.

Annoyed

_____.

Annoyed — rude

_____.

Annoyed — rude — remarks

_____.

Defeat

_____.

Defeat — debate

_____.

Defeat — debate — disappointed

_____.

Ⅱ Practice the key patterns

T: come to this town

S1: Did you come to this town before?

S2: No. This is the first time I have come to this town.

Practice: (1) visit the Great Wall

(2) go for a trip by air

(3) have a blind date

(4) bake the cake

T: have dinner — my friend comes

S1: Have you had dinner?

S2: Not yet. I will have dinner when my friend comes.

Practice: (1) go to the park — the rain stops

(2) clean the living room — I am free

(3) repair the fence — it is sunny

(4) give Uncle Wang a call — I get home

T: work in a law office — enter this company

S1: What did you do before you enter this company?

S2: I had been working in a law office for a year before entering this company.

Practice: (1) study in Peking University — get this job

(2) work in a automobile company — go abroad

(3) teach English in a college — become a middle school teacher

Ⅲ Retell the story

Firstly complete the blanks and remember what you said.

A Festival for the Dead is held once a year in Japan. This festival is _____, for on this day, the dead are said to _____ and they are welcomed by the living. As they are expected to be hungry after their long journey, food is _____. Specially-made lanterns are hung outside each house to _____. All night long, people dance and sing. In the early morning, the food that had been laid out for the dead is _____ as it is considered _____

_____. In towns that are near the sea, the tiny lanterns which had been hung in the streets the night before, are placed into the water when the festival is over. Thousands of lanterns _____

_____ on their return journey to the other world. This is

_____, for crowds of people _____

_____ until they can be seen no more.

Secondly retell the story in the third person.

Ⅳ Active questions

1. What is held once a year in Japan?
2. Why is it a cheerful occasion?
3. Why is food laid out for them?
4. What are hung outside each house?
5. What do people do all night long?
6. Why food is thrown away in the morning?
7. What do people believe that these lanterns can do?
8. Why is this a moving spectacle?

Ⅴ Translate the following sentences into English

1. 她以讽刺的口吻回答了我的提问。
2. 我更愿意在国内发展我的事业。
3. 实验证明，梦是现实的反映。
4. 小的时候他常常中午去捉知了。

5. 那一幕在她心中留下了深刻的印象。

6. 谁都有犯错的时候，重要的是要及时改正。

7. 他入伍已经有 8 个春秋了。

8. 酒后驾车容易发生交通事故。

9. 他一直在期待暑假的来临。

10. 到最后他们都对这场考试失去了信心。

千淘万漉　吹尽黄沙

21 世纪是个信息时代，语言作为人类信息、沟通、交流的基本工具，是我们一直在坚持不肯放弃的！而英语作为全球第一语言，覆盖世界各地，当英语的重要性一点点被彰显出来的时候，"英语热"随之而兴起。英语学习已经成为中国和世界接轨的一种趋势。

在这种大的背景之下，英语培训机构应运而生。其中，行业英语培训、口语培训以及口语翻译培训在英语培训市场中占据了较大的份额，英语口语人才需求量更是猛增。作为中国华电集团公司直属部门单位的中国华电高级培训中心，具有非常得天独厚的央企背景和品牌优势。"智慧英语"以此为依托，以"好口语、好人生"为培训目标，以"重培训品牌、重培训服务、重培训质量"为培训精神，在赢得广大客户的信赖的同时，依据自身优势，进一步完善教学方式，诚信服务，从而在众多的培训机构中脱颖而出。

"智慧英语"的信念是以精良的教师服务和客服团队为每名学员提供自由化、人性化的优质教学服务。其温馨融洽的学习氛围，独到的培训特点、授课特点，成为众多培训客户选择的对象！

没有千淘万漉的艰辛，怎会有吹尽黄沙始到金的喜悦。选择智慧英语，您对您的人生负责，我们对您的英语负责！

华电智慧英语培训班报名回执表

姓名		英文名		出生年月	
性别		毕业院校		学历	
专业		毕业时间 英语级别		工作单位	
职务		家庭住址址		联系电话	
个人培训 意向	具体培训课程请参看 www. wisdomenglish. net				
团体培训 意向（请 根据自己 的需求在 相应的行 业标注）	旅游＋拓展		商务英语		
	计算机		接待英语		
	银行		软件英语		
	电力科普		医疗		
	法律		建筑		

注意事项：1. 培训者认真填写表格，写明详细信息

2. "个人培训意向"请参看网站

3. 将填好的表格剪下，邮寄或发电子邮件至报名地点中国华电集团高级培训中心外语培训部"智慧英语连锁机构"

地址：北京市密云县鼓楼东大街富民新区 1－13 号

邮政编码：101512

电话：010－69027385 010－69088520

传真：010－69027385

E-mail: wisdomenglish@163. com